D1255669

THE HOLOCAUST KID

THE HOLOCAUST KID

Stories

SONIA PILCER

A Karen and Michael Braziller Book

PERSEA BOOKS/NEW YORK

Some of the stories and poems in *The Holocaust Kid* have appeared previously, in different versions, in the following publications: *Ann Arbor Review, 7 Days, Baltimore Jewish Times, Jerusalem Post, The Forward, New York Post, The Voice of Piotrkow Survivors, Auschwitz: Beginning of a New Era* (KTAV, 1976), *Visions of America: Personal Narratives from the Promised Land* (Persea Books, 1993), *New York Sex* (Painted Leaf Press, 1998).

Requests for permission to reprint or to make copies and for any other information should be addressed to the publisher:

Persea Books, Inc.
171 Madison Avenue
New York, New York 10016

Library of Congress Cataloging-in-Publication Data
Pilcer, Sonia.
    The Holocaust kid : a novel / Sonia Pilcer.—1st U.S. ed.
        p. cm
    "A Karen and Michael Braziller book."
    ISBN 0-89255-261-1 (cloth : alk. paper)
    1. Children of Holocaust survivors—Fiction. 2. Jews—New York (State)—New York—Fiction. 3. Jewish families—Fiction. 4. New York (N.Y.)—Fiction. 5. Women authors—Fiction. I. Title.

PS3566.I48 H65 2001
813'.54—dc21

                                    20010221297

Manufactured in the United States of America

Designed by Rita Lascaro

FIRST EDITION

For my parents

Lusia Gradon Pilcer & Benjamin Pilcer

Acknowledgments

My parents' circle of survivors have surrounded my life. I feel privileged to be among their scribes.

I wish to acknowledge Carl D. Brandt and Diane Cleaver, who was representing *The Holocaust Kid* at the time of her death.

Many read this book during its nearly twenty-year gestation. I am especially grateful to Susie Kaufman and Catherine Hiller.

Rabbi Bob Gluck showed me a way back to Judaism, which, of course, is part of this story too.

Thank you, Gareth Esersky and Karen Braziller, for taking on the challenge.

Finally, I wish to express gratitude for family: my husband Morton Makler and our son, Jacob Pilcer Makler.

The Virginia Center of Creative Arts offered me fellowship and a well-lit place to work.   —S.P.

Yours is a privileged generation: you remember things that you have not lived; but you remember them so well, so profoundly, that every one of your words, every one of your stories, every one of your silences comes to bear on our own. You are our justification.

—Elie Wiesel
First International Conference of
Children of Holocaust Survivors, May 1984

CONTENTS

THE HOLOCAUST KID

DO YOU DESERVE TO LIVE?

"I'm proud to be a Jew," Elizabeth Taylor declared, pledging $100,000 in war bonds for Israel. She had converted to Judaism to marry Eddie Fisher, who called her his "Yiddena," his little Jewish woman.

"I feel as if I've been a Jew all my life," she exulted, dark lashes sweeping over the famed violet eyes. Draped in Beverly Hills crepe, a deep Prussian blue, her head veiled like a biblical matriarch, she was once again the beautiful Rebecca in *Ivanhoe*.

"I felt terribly sorry for the suffering of the Jews during the war. I was attracted to their heritage. I guess I identified with them as underdog."

"Makes her furious," Richard Burton quipped years later. "I tell her, 'You're not Jewish at all.' She turns white with rage."

/ / /

1972. I was managing editor of *Movie Screen,* the magazine of the stars. When I wasn't doing what I thought of as my real work, penning blood-eyed poems in a blue-lined notebook, I edited stories, composed captions for the gossip pix, calling Celebrity Service several times a day to check facts like the names and ages of Tom Jones's children.

On my desk, there was a gold-framed photograph of a baby posed like a Spanish infanta, crowned with a white satin bonnet, its sash tied in a bow. The dress is a marvel of white satin with lace on the collar and bodice, puffed sleeves from which two plump arms unfold. But it's the eyes that amazed my mother's friends in Landsberg, the Displaced Persons camp, where I was born.

"Such eyes. The very spitten image of Elisabet Tailor," declared Gita Blum, who had survived eight months of Auschwitz. Her numbers flashed like blue neon on her bejeweled arm.

"Genia, when you get to America, you must take Zosha to Hollywood. Get her a *scream* test," insisted Mushka Schransky. She had lived as a Christian maid for the family of an SS soldier. "I tell you, she could be movie star."

Shocking cover lines sold *Movie Screen*. My editor, Flavia O'Neal, a whiskey-drinking Irishwoman with thick black brows, intense eyes, was NYU Journalism '57. She came up with the hard-hitting, newslike headlines and bought sleazy photographs from paparazzi. Our sleight-of-hand was to "justify" the headline, the more deliciously sinful the implication, the greater the triumph of the con: i.e., my very own "Cher's Secret Hours in the Dark with Robert Redford." (She attended a premiere of his latest film.)

This was years before *People* published real dirt. Someone had to create it.

In the back of the magazine were ads that promised a panacea: firm chin muscles; increase your bustline by five full inches; be taller instantly; eat the foods you crave and love, yet lose lumpy, fatty excess weight; cover up ugly veins; unwanted hair gone; remove blackheads in seconds; and the satin porn of Frederick's of Hollywood with its peek-a-boo nipple bras, "sinsuous" slinks, and open- fanny panties. And in the front, our galaxy of stars.

"I want to discuss something with you," my mother stated, holding open the *Daily News* in two hands. "Serious." Her tone was grave, like when she was going to read me a story about a Holocaust survivor who was reunited with her sister or a Nazi found living in Floral Gardens. I was eight.

"Debbie Reynolds was America's sweetheart," Genia said, pointing to a small photograph of a pert young woman with a flip, inserted over a huge, four-color spread of Elizabeth Taylor. "The girl next-to-door. Debbie was married to Eddie Fisher. A Jew. The stars aren't religious, so they intermarry. No matter. He sang 'My Yiddishe Mama.' Remember him on television?"

I turned to my mother, who had laid down the newspaper on the kitchen table next to my multiplication tables, which I was trying to memorize. "Mom, I have to do my homework."

"Anyway, Liz is a beautiful woman," she continued, ignoring me. "The most beautiful in the world. What a shame." My mother shook her head sadly. "I hate to say this. Especially because you have her eyes, everyone says so, even when you were a baby. That's why it breaks my heart to talk about this. But you have to know the truth."

I stared at my multiplication tables. *Nine times nine equals eighty-one.*

"You're too young to know what a housebreaker is. It's a woman who steals the husband of another woman, making him leave his children, his happy home. For what? A moment's pleasure? This is what Elizabeth Taylor has done. Sure, she was upset about Mike Todd dying. He was a good man, the only man she ever loved. She divorced that Nicky Hilton guy. He was a drunk. Such a thing? How can she do it? Debbie just had a baby and now there's another one on the way. Liz doesn't care about nobody but herself."

What we at the magazine had to do was whip up a pastiche on the themes of money and misery, the curse of being beautiful and/or talented, and how success and fame can never be a substitute for love. The *Movie Screen* Bible stated: "We give them courtship, weddings, babies, divorces, illness, and sex. But the most important thing, remember: the stars are just like you and me, only more so."

Only a few stars, maybe half a dozen, actually sold movie fan magazines. There had to be something larger than life that transcended time and personal tragedy, inspiring the most passionate, undying loyalty or just simple adoration. And Elizabeth Taylor was still queen.

Mort Jacobs, legal counsel for Flame Publishing, checked out manuscripts, refusing to let copy through unless, point by point, the story delivered—without any real slander, which recent suits had proved were costly. He had surprised us by rejecting a cover story by one of our regulars. So yours truly, Dr. Shlock, had to take over at zero hour, breathing life into one of the genre's oldest diddles, trying to reach the punchline with a minimum of moans and guffaws from her reader. I was not only reigning high priestess of low journalism, but also the fastest emergency writer in movie fanzinedom. My specialty: vulnerability stories—movie stars have feelings too—taking on the occasional true confession or soap story, but nonpareil on Liz, my altered ego.

Feeding a sheet of bond into the electric Olympia, black carbon flagging behind, I typed the headline: *THE LOVE-CHILD LIZ TAYLOR WILL NOT ACKNOWLEDGE AS HER OWN.* Dropping several lines, I added the heart-clenching subhead: *How It Has Destroyed Her Marriage! Liz Cries: "God, Can You Ever Forgive Me?"*

Lighting a cigarette, I summoned my shlock muse. O muse, so tacky, bless me with the silken tongue to touch the ghettos of the human heart. To bamboozle them with the promise of sin, titillate their yens, give succor to their delusions.

Come to me in your rhinestone harlequin glasses, cabana pants, and spiked heels. Get started, Hedda Hophead. Go on! Suck into the metaphysic of star worship, its temples, corner drugstores. and laundromats, altars of the washer and dryer. I could feel it like an orgasm. Soon I would be the voice of female longing in America, aching after the famous, the ass-sucked and arrogant, cannibalizing them to satisfy her readers' hunger.

"Do it, goddamn it!" I crushed my cigarette in the shell ashtray. Cover unsightly stretch marks; longer, thicker hair in ten minutes; look twenty years younger.

/　/　/

The sun streaked through a splinter of an opening in the royal blue drapes of Liz's opulent bedroom. She tried to shield her sleep-filled violet eyes, instinctively flinging her arm to reach out for her husband, but the pain of memory surfaced: he was gone. Richard had walked out on her. A shiver ran down her spine, chilling her though it was a balmy June morning. Memory was a tidal wave sweeping her in its whirlpool of images.

Suddenly, the stench of burning! I watched with fascination as a small transparent crescent fried in the ashtray, folding into itself as it singed. Picking it up, I discovered it was human in its stickiness. It was my own fingernail, clipped some days ago, now fixed to the tip of my finger.

"Ugh!" I recoiled, trying to flick the singed nail off one finger, but it stuck to the other finger. That's how they burned. I grabbed my notebook.

> *Like burnt crust*
> *in a frying pan*
> *you stuck to the edges.*

> *You had to be*
> *scraped out*
> *hair by tender hair*

Stop it. Liz! Liz! Liz! "Fuck the art!" Richard Burton had raved. "I want to be rich, rich, rich." The story was due at four. I stuck the notebook back in my desk drawer. My fingers lined up on the typewriter keys like a firing squad, the cash register of words per dollar ringing at the end of each line.

/ / /

Liz wished she could share her terrible secret with one of her friends. It might relieve the burden of her guilt. But she was not one to open her pain and anguish to others. She buried it deep within her soul . . .

I was writing and then I wasn't, finding myself wondering instead: Would I have survived? How did a person live from day to day? Would I have traded my body for bread? Fucked Nazis? What would I do with my desire to die? With my impatience? My impulsiveness? What would I do with my fears? Do you deserve to live?

"Write!" I cried out. "Enough with the introspection!"

At that moment, Christine peeked in from the doorway. "I heard that. You know, I read somewhere that people who live by themselves talk to themselves." She occupied the office next to *Movie Screen* and had the exact same job, except her magazine was *MovieLand*.

"Okay, Chris. The twenty-four-thousand-dollar question. How would you write '*The Love-Child Liz Taylor Will Not Acknowledge as Her Own'?*"

"Her grandson, of course," Christine suggested, twisting her long red braid around her hand.

"We did that story with Jackie two months ago," I told her.

"How about 'the child within herself,' who was never allowed to grow up like a normal little girl . . . " Christine began.

"A star at eight, famous at such a tender age," I continued in my best Hollywood tragedy voice. "She had fans by the millions, rode in limousines."

"But what she didn't have—" Christine crooned.

"—was a sense of being loved for her self."

"—And she never had a childhood," Christine concluded. "So now she must go back and acknowledge that child who was never allowed to grow up." She grinned at me. "I wrote that story about Ann-Margret."

"Hey, no one ever accused us of originality."

Christine was an English major like me, two years out of college. Shared contempt for fan magazines and our mutual sense of each other's greater destinies united us. She lived with an Italian sculptor in a loft on Wooster Street.

The phone rang. I let it ring until a machine picked up. "Listen, Chris," I began.

Her eyes met mine. "*Ciao,* darling. Send Liz my best."

It started like a migraine. The blue haze before the assault. Silent, cruel, insidious accusations. Did we survive the war for this? Sleaze? You think you're a real writer? Shlockmeister. Try standing in the freezing snow for two hours without shoes.

What about my years of scribbling in notebooks? I protested meekly. The poems. My files. The self-proclaimed poetess. What a hoot. I had found my calling with Liz and Dick, and like a wedding cake pair, they crowned my fondest aspirations. *Just write the damn story!*

Affliction stamps the soul to its very depths with the scorn, the disgust and even the self-hatred and sense of guilt that crime logically should produce but actually does not.
                                                                    —*Simone Weil*

What I wanted, why I yearned to be a writer was to tell stories. My parents' stories, which were mine too. Slowly, I slid open my desk drawer, pulling out a manila folder. I had printed one word on the cover. SURVIVORS.

The first story was about a young girl whose life was saved by a white scarf. Her parents and baby brother were sent to a death camp, while she was selected for a work *lager*.

In the second story, a religious boy survived Auschwitz. He never saw his parents or his two sisters again. He escaped while an officer peed in the woods.

And I, their daughter, live in two time frames. Normal, shared reality: everyone stops at the red light. The other zone has no temporal sense. Burnt by a dog-eared yellow star, sign of the Jew, rising, hungry eyes, overripe crazylegs nerve. I live in the ghetto of the dead.

The phone rang again. I didn't pick it up. No interruptions while working! Then I pressed the red button on my phone machine. "Are you there? Are you there?" My mother's Polish-accented voice. "I *von't* speak to a machine. Zosha, call your momma right away."

Shut the folder. Return it to the drawer. I picked up the receiver. My mother's phone was busy. I tried again. Still busy. Always busy. A flibbertigibbet. I could see her sitting at the kitchen table, fruit-and-vegetable wallpaper whirling around her. She wound the phone cord around her wrist as she spoke her musical Polish. Now she was doing the dishes as she talked. It was dangerous to be idle, even for a moment. The yellow wall phone jerked as she moved around with the long cord following like a leash.

Finally, she picked up. On the first ring. "I knew it was you!" she rejoiced, then her voice became critical. "What took so long?"

"You were busy."

"It's true. I was talking to Stella Brumstein. You remember her?"

"Did you call for any reason?"

"I hate that *meshuggeh* machine! Do I have to have a reason to call my own daughter?" She paused, then began again. "I never hear from you. You don't call—"

"I'm calling you right now."

"Because I called you."

"Mother, let's stop this."

"I don't know anything about your life. Are you—uh—seeing—" she inquired hopefully, "someone?"

"No one special."

"Someone not so special then. He doesn't have to be Prince Charming. Though people always say how good-looking is your father. Do you go out on dates?"

She knew about Ludwig, the German guy I was dating, but pretended he didn't exist. I had brought him home for a disastrous dinner some months before, and neither of us had mentioned him since. "I'm at work," I insisted. "I can't have this conversation."

"Zosha, I don't see why you can't find someone. All my friends have already grandchildren and what do I have? *Bupkes.*"

"Mom, I'm hanging up!"

Seemingly chastened, her tone turned grave. "I called about something important."

"Okay."

"Yom Hashoah is a week from Sunday."

I didn't say anything.

"The day when we remember the Holocaust."

"I know what Yom Hashoah is."

"We bought you a ticket. It's at Temple Emanu-El on Fifth Avenue," she continued. "You know, that fancy *shul* with the rich people."

"Mom, I have plans—"

"And what could more important than Yom Hashoah?" she demanded. "You must come. Everyone will be there. The Mayor always comes. Senator Javits. Theodore Bikel. Lots of celebrities too."

"I wish you had told me sooner," I said, trying to think of a worthy excuse. Something she'd accept. "I have to—"

"Zosha, for us." Her voice heavy. My stomach twisted, the gnarled torso of an ancient tree. "Please do it," she implored.

"I don't know," I said. "I'll try—"

"We've bought you a seat," she stated conclusively. "Twelve noon sharp." Then added, "Could you wear the dress I sewed for you? It so brings out your eyes."

"Sure," I surrendered weakly.

"Okay, I know you're a busy lady. But I've been thinking on a totally different subject. And you can tell me if you don't want to do it . . . " Her voice trailed off. "Okay?"

"Yes?" I held the receiver from my ear.

"You know how you have to make up names for those stories you write for the magazine?"

"Mom," I resisted. "What do you want? I have to finish a story today."

"I know that. But I was just thinking about something. Why should you make the names up of the writers from the air?"

"We all use pseudonyms."

"It's a pity you don't use your name so everyone will know what a wonderful writer you are. I show my friends the magazine and say, 'This one my Zosha wrote.' I'm so proud, but to be honest, I don't know if they even believe me. Who's this Louise Colet? It doesn't say anywhere—"

I broke in. "Mom, I don't want my name attached to this magazine."

"Such a big shot she's become! They're good stories about Elizabeth Taylor, Elvis Pretsley, Jackie O—with human feelings. Of course, I never bring such magazines in the house, but in America, everyone reads them at the beauty parlor."

"I don't want—"

"So all right. You don't want. But I was talking to Gita Blum. You know her, with the daughter Bella, a little fat but with a pretty face, who goes to Queens College. And I don't know if you know, but before the war, she wrote very nice poems and stories."

"Yes, yes—" I said impatiently.

"Not even a moment for your mommy?"

"I've got to go." My voice was becoming ugly, the one I hated. After all the resolutions: *What she went through, how she suffered. I could never have survived. I mustn't make my mother suffer more.*

"Anyway, I'll be Speedy Gonzalez since you've become such an important person," she said. "We were talking and she asked me if you wouldn't mind using her name for one of the stories. That way she could see her name in print. I mean, of course, if you use your name, that's something else. But if you're going to make up Louise Colet, why not Fela Brumstein? Or even, for that matter, why not Genia Radon?"

At first, Liz swore to herself that she would never tell him about her child, afraid that it would destroy her marriage. How she cried nights as he slept peacefully! "God, can you ever forgive me?" She prayed in the silence of the night. Finally, she could no longer keep it inside of herself. Richard had to know the truth. But would he ever come back to her?

/ / /

Eventually all my stories were signed with the names of my mother's Polski platoon. But my most frequent pseudonym—once even receiving a note from a befuddled Glenn Ford thanking her for a stimulating interview, which, of course, never took place except in my imagination—was Genia Radon, my mother's maiden name.

DISPLACED PERSONS

I am especially happy to be in a Jewish camp on the holiest day of your year. For the time being, you are here and you must be patient until the day comes when you can leave for whatever destination is yours. The U.S. Army is here to help you. And it must rest with you to maintain good order and friendly relations with the established authorities. I know how much you have suffered and I believe there is still a bright day ahead for you.

—General Dwight David Eisenhower
Landsberg, Germany
September 1945

Genia wheeled a baby carriage past the gray military barracks of "the Miracle of Landsberg." Though it was better than the Berlin camp, where they had lived for six months after leaving Poland, it was still no paradise. She and Heniek had been in Landsberg for four years, waiting for papers to come to America.

After the war, these camps sheltered thousands of "displaced persons," refugees whose families had been killed. They had nowhere to go. Most had little in common except memories that haunted them and gnawing desperation, speaking a Babel of tongues, and more kept arriving. Some were very sick. But they were young and recuperated quickly. Children who had found each other during the war continued to run together like packs of mongrels. Couples still mourning dead spouses and murdered children were marrying again in improvised ceremonies. Pregnant women waddled with huge bellies. Babies sprang up everywhere. Landsberg had one of the biggest baby booms in history.

The American Jewish Joint Committee, committed to "rebuilding Jewish lives and Jewish life," aided Landsberg with its own hospital, orphanage, and nursery. There was a library, a synagogue with a Talmud printed on German soil and inscribed in Hebrew, "From Slavery to Redemption." There were cooking and tailoring classes, trade schools, even a kibbutz with an agricultural training center for Zionists who would emigrate to Palestine. Youth and sports groups competed, theater and orchestras performed in the social hall, where American movies were shown weekly.

As Genia walked by the barbed-wire gate, she passed a handwritten sign: TRADING HELPS THE GERMANS AND ONLY BLACKENS THE JEWISH NAME.

The city of Landsberg was just outside the camp. Stately old German houses, painted brown and white with red cobbled roofs, butchers, tailor shops, *konditerai* with all kinds of sweets, cafes and restaurants, mountains on the horizon.

What Genia noticed, though, were the others like herself. DPs, refugees from death and disease, who wore similar dresses, having received surplus fabrics from America. DPs walked with stiff postures down the street but turned around frequently, as if pursued, anticipating attack, arrest for an unmentionable crime, or perhaps being found by a loved one who by some perverse quirk lives. Genia looked straight ahead, her mouth pursed against hope.

Thema Rosenkrantz discovered her sister, Esther, long thought dead, at the *Tausgescheft*. She had come for salt. Esther was trading a chipped teapot for vinegar. Thema began to scream. Her dark hair was blond so Esther did not recognize her, and she had grown fat. Suddenly, she knew her sister. Dropping the glass bottle of vinegar, she ran to embrace her. You could smell vinegar for days.

Genia wheeled her carriage past German mothers with their baby carriages. Genia sidled up to them, close, as if inviting intimacy. She complimented the unsuspecting mother as she peered inside the woman's carriage—the beauty of her baby, the fineness of her embroidery stitch. Glowing, the German woman was proud. Only then did Genia lure her to her own carriage. She stood back to observe the effect. How she exulted in that moment! That it could last forever! The surprise on the woman's face! Stunned, the mother clutched the edge of Genia's carriage, abandoning her own for several moments.

"What a beauty! Exquisite. The eyes—" Genia dropped her eyes modestly. "Like the mother."

"They gasp," she said after the woman walked away, "At the sight of you, my miracle. They lose their breath. Oh, you're going to have a blessed life." She sighed loudly. "Not like your momma's."

The old clock in the stone tower struck two. The archway below it led to Augsburgstrasse.

So much sadness and loss. But now Genia has her reward. Zosha's photograph, the biggest picture in such an expensive golden frame, in the window of Herr Kruger's photo shop.

She peered into the window and only incidentally caught her own reflection, admiring her teeth. "My little one," she whispered. "No one has eyes like you, although everyone admires mine too. Eyes are so important. After a while, they were all I recognized when I saw my face."

Genia thought of the photograph on her father's roll-top desk. It showed her handsome mother, Zosia, with thick dark hair heaped in an upswept hairdo; dignified, stuffy Tata, her father, with his pompous mustache, pince-nez, and carved meerschaum pipe. Baby brother Jesse's girlish brown curls uncut over his plump face. And Genia, the spoiled *gymnazium* student in the pleated skirt, white blouse, and navy blazer with her Jewish school's emblem. Genia's expression was serious, unsmiling, because her teeth were crooked.

Herr Kruger stepped outside, startling Genia. "Frau Palovsky, you come to look at the picture again? Some people ask about it."

"Is that so?" she asked softly.

"Yes. Actually today a woman walked in, who was it? I forget. But she said your daughter looks like that child actress in American movies. What is her name?"

Genia took a deep breath. "Try to remember. Please, Herr Kruger."

"I don't know American movies."

"Was it by any chance—Elisabet Tailor?"

He paused thoughtfully. "Yes. I think that's the one. Such a pretty girl, your Zosha." He leaned over the carriage. "May I?" He started to lift the veil.

"No!" Genia cried out in horror. "The baby is sleeping, Herr Kruger."

He drew back. "Excuse me."

"Oh, no." Genia tried to mollify him. "It's just that she wasn't well in the morning."

"I'm so sorry. And now?"

"Like a piece of gold." She paused for a moment. "Herr Kruger, I was wondering if you could be so kind as to give me one more copy of the picture—for my uncle in America—"

"Frau Palovsky, I've already given you half a dozen. Out of my own pocket, which I have to pay for—"

"But you yourself said that people come into your shop and ask—" she implored, her eyes meeting his, unrelenting. "You know, after the war, it is all I have, so little—"

He shook his head pitifully. "It's very difficult for all of us now. We lost family too. My brother, Ulrich, was a Communist. They took him to Dachau."

"I'm so sorry." She waited a moment, then asked, "Just one photograph?"

"For you, I'll make two. But no more."

She offered him her loveliest smile. "Thank you."

After returning inside, he turned to look at her. She remained standing outside.

"He thinks he can touch you, just like that, with his gentile fingers. I'll never let anyone harm you."

Genia bent over the carriage, lifted the veil, picking up the baby.

"That's you, darling. Can you see? In the center. Look, will you!" She stepped closer to the window. As she spoke her breath steamed the glass. "Did you hear what the man said? Someone told it to him. In America, they have a movie star who is a child. Elisabet Tailor. I knew it when they showed the film in the camp. *Nation Velvet*. Such a strange name, no? She could be your sister. The same eyes and hair. I swear it. Do you see? Pay attention, Zosha. Right there, in the gold frame. Next to the nothing bride."

The baby reached out to touch the hard and shiny glass. She left five dots like a paw mark. Above it, Genia traced Z-O-S-H-A in the steam. As it unwrote itself in a broken string of pearls, she sighed. "As I stand here, I just know it. Your life will be special."

Herr Kruger watched as the young mother crossed the street, wheeling the carriage. His eyes followed until she turned the corner. He took out a plaid handkerchief, fresh with the smell of bleach, and wiped his face. Shaking his head, he walked back into the back of his store to search for the negatives of the baby's portrait.

"To the post office, Zosha, before it closes. Maybe there's a letter," Genia said. From someone she hasn't thought of. Forgotten. Resurrected from ashes, eyeglasses smashed, her father's were gold-rimmed, slipping down his face as he fell asleep over *Nowa Gazeta*. A check from HIAS, the Hebrew Immigrant Aid Society.

She stood in line with the carriage. There were many ahead of her. And only one clerk, a young German with wire-framed glasses, sheets of paper wrapped around each of his cuffs with rubber bands. So neat, the Germans. He was slow and stupid, fumbling through stacks of letters. As she waited, she began to fidget, staring toward the front of the line. It was so far away. How she hated to stand in lines. They should never make her endure this again after all the lines, for runny soup of turnip and potato peels, her crust of bread, to go to the *pushka*, when they allowed her. And now she must wait again. How can they do this to her? Don't they know? There should be a special line for those who suffered. How she watched Momma, Tata, her baby brother, Jesse, stolen from her. How a freak of a predilection, her mother's white kerchief, saved her life.

Genia stared at the others ahead of her. Germans. A young woman, about her age, wearing a good woolen suit. Did she wipe toilets? Subsist on garbage? And what of the gentleman in front of her who holds his hat in his hand? Such a gentleman with such good manners. Was he so well-mannered when he informed on a Jewish business to be rewarded in kind? Her father's shop—even the mayor's deputy came to buy material for a new suit before the war. And the elderly man. How many Nazis did he raise? How much she hated, wishing cholera to overcome every last one of them, so they'd die violent, undignified deaths like everyone she loved.

Mustn't think these things, she scolded herself. Madness lay there like a soft bed. Mirka Abramson was taken to the hospital because her nightmares woke everyone in the barracks. Even afternoons, the sun an unbroken yolk outside the window, she wouldn't stop screaming.

Finally. Genia gave her name, pronouncing slowly so that he would understand. "P-A-L-O-V-S-K-Y. P like

Piotrkow." He leafed through the stack of P's. "American Zone," she added quietly. He looked up at her, curious as a viper.

"Frau Palovsky, Heniek?" he asked, holding a letter with an official stamp on the envelope.

"Yes, this is me," she answered in her halting German Yiddish.

She handed him her identity card. He returned it to her, with the letter. She wheeled the carriage to a corner where she ripped open the envelope in alarm.

Immediately, she spotted the words GENERAL HERSEY. Bremenhaven. To leave on the ship, *General Hersey*. United States of America. She lost her breath. Permission to go to America. It had come. . . .

America of refrigerators that light up like a theater with every kind of food to imagine, hot running water, and bathtubs like swimming pools. Private toilets too. Saving money, waiting to be sponsored. Genia had even sewn a jacket with padded shoulders exactly like Barbara Stanwyck's.

As she walked home, the letter folded in the zippered compartment of her pocketbook, she began her packing. Seeing herself wrap each precious piece of the Rosenthal china set in newspaper. Her Pfaff sewing machine with leg pedal. Her meat grinder, her black iron pots, the silver menorah. There was no weight limit. Her featherbed and down pillows, folding the double-button blanket cover, her embroidered pillowcases, the lace tablecloth, and the kitchen towels.

Genia gazed down into the carriage. "We're going to America," she whispered excitedly, bending over to adjust the baby's blanket.

She found her way back to the old stone tower. Half past three. Soon Heniek will be home.

Genia wheeled the carriage past the sign, TRADING HELPS THE GERMANS AND ONLY BLACKENS THE JEWISH NAME, into the camp.

Inside the barracks, a thin wall separated their part from the Haupsteins and their two boys. Immediately, Genia was nauseated by the stench of Rena's soup, bratwurst and cabbage. Worse than the *hasag!* And her nagging voice, which was loud and crude. Genia knocked on the wall. "Please, can you be a little quiet? My Zosha is sleeping."

For a moment, there was silence. Then Rena said so everyone could hear, "Who does she think she is, Pani Palovsky with her airs? I don't care who your father was and your stinking apartment on Mokotowska. You're here and have the same nothing we have."

Genia wouldn't answer her, the pig who is common. America! America! She chanted the magic word as she carried the big iron pot to the coal-burning stove. "We'll have our own apartment with a private toilet," she whispered.

She lifted the baby gently, placing her on their mattress. "Did you make a *kaka*?" She checked the diaper. "No! What a good girl. We'll try later but first, *mleko*. You must be hungry, my little blue eyes."

She unbuttoned her flowered shift. All the women have such dresses because HIAS gave them the material from America. But hers with pearl buttons was the finest. Mother taught her how to sew, the silver needle darting in and out of her lap like a dragonfly. Genia stepped out of the dress, in just her silk slip, blue as the veins in Heniek's strong arms and legs. If no one knew, she knew that it was real silk against her skin, even if the flowered dresses walked all over Landsberg. She unhooked her brassiere, then picked the baby up, drawing her to her right breast with its swollen nipple. It was fat with milk.

"Drink, my love," she crooned, easing her nipple into the baby's mouth.

Genia imagined a cave of tongue and teeth. A body of water waiting for the diver to split its mirrored skin. Heniek! So handsome. A jet of warmth shot through her body. Rena was screaming at her husband, Bolek, but she no longer heard. Mother and daughter were lost in each other's embrace. White, milky bliss.

A man could, of course, enter. Sometimes he did, the stranger, the one who traveled and traded money, counting in guttural Yiddish. He was always dark. Often he bore gifts. Now there was only the island of skin, the fields of nippled milk.

Afterward, the baby chortled with Genia's lovely soprano. Drawing her hands together, she sang, "Clap hands, clap hands till Daddy comes home. Daddy has money and Momma has none. Clap hands, clap hands."

While she peeled carrots, sliced onions to add to yesterday's stew, how he likes, the baby played on the rug she had woven from rags.

When she finished, she lifted the baby up. "Time for you to show Momma what a big girl you are."

The baby sat dumbly on the wooden baby seat, looking around as Genia made straining sounds to give her the idea.

"You're lucky you have a toilet. Look, how clean and easy. I had to make in a can, when they let me."

The baby began to bounce restlessly, kicking her legs. Genia tightened her grip. "You're not going anywhere." She shook her. "I won't change diapers in America."

Zosha began to cry. "Oh no!" Genia picked her up, kissing her legs, and placed her gently into her crib.

Good. Zosha lay quiet. Heniek's stew on a low fire. Genia took out the basket of strawberries. *Truskawki!* A sinful amount she paid at the market, but they'd dazzled her. Spending her pin money so she could have them. He'd be angry. She emptied several perfect berries into a white bowl, hiding the basket behind the wardrobe where it was cool. She rinsed them, then sprinkled sugar like snow so they would bleed their thick syrup. Being truly wicked, she pulled out her left breast, the one that Zosha neglected, squeezing her nipple until the milk frothed, spraying into the bowl of strawberries. Red, succulent. Tasting sweeter because she knows it is her own milk. Greedily, she sucked the roundness, then bit into the berry, its juice sluicing inside her mouth. Oh, good, good. Errant drops like rubies.

Just then, she heard his steps outside. Doesn't want to stop but doesn't want him to know her secret. He'll crush it with the heel of his shoe. No time, no money for such stupid things. So she swallowed them whole and they were gone, the berries whole in her belly like precious stones.

Heniek entered silently, hanging up his brown corduroy jacket, worn at the elbows, the pockets stretched so they flapped unhappily.

She noticed but said nothing. Instead, she threw her arms around his neck girlishly.

"Heniek, I have such good news—" she began excitedly.

He walked over to the stove, warming his hands. "Is supper ready?"

The stew! She had forgotten. Running to the stove, she

lifted the lid. "Oh, no!" She screamed, dropping it. The lid crashed on the floor.

"What's the matter with you? Can't you make a decent meal without burning it? What else did you have to do today?"

"But I have such news. Wait until you hear!"

"I don't care about any news now. I'm hungry. Understand? I've been working since six in the morning. *Chleb!*"

"Yes, yes. Just a moment." She took out a loaf from the breadbox. "Look, fresh from the baker. Smell how fresh. Rye bread, you wanted."

He snatched the loaf from her, breaking off a piece with his hands.

"Wait! What are you doing? Use a knife, Heniek."

He bit into the thick piece, teeth like fangs. "What about the meat?"

"I only have two hands. Just a minute."

"I don't see what you have better to do that you can't prepare my supper so I can have it when I come home and not have to beg for my food. Is that too much to ask?"

Genia placed a plate with stew before him. "Only the bottom burnt," she said softly.

He dipped the bread into the sauce, slurping as he chewed with his mouth open.

She carried a plate for herself and sat down next to him.

"Did you have a good day?" she asked.

He shrugged, shoulders heavy as bricks.

"Today I went to the post office—" she began again but he was rapt, his passion inside his plate. He tore off another piece of bread, wiping the curved rim with the crust. She had stopped eating and watched as the gravy ran down his chin. Finally, she said, "I wish you would use the knife."

He pushed the meat with the bread into his mouth.

"It's only good manners," she added.

"Let *them* have *their* good manners. I'll eat in my own home how I feel like it." To punctuate his words, he banged on the table with the bread knife.

"Don't," she urged "The baby . . . "

His eyes gladdened as if he had suddenly remembered. "My little girl!" Swallowing the meat-soaked piece of bread, he rushed over to the crib. "Asleep like a challah. Come on, say hello to your daddy." He leaned over to pick up the baby.

Genia tried to pull him away. "She just fell asleep, Heniek."

"The only time I ever see her, she's sleeping. I want to play with my daughter." His arms reached into the crib. The animals began to spin. "Look, she has a dimple in her chin like her father."

"Heniek, don't you want to finish supper?"

He picked up the baby gently, unsure of how to hold such a creature, so small. But warm and soft. He ran his fingers over the white down on her face. "Like a kitten," he whispered. "The fingers with their tiny nails."

Startled, the baby began to cry.

"Don't cry, *kindeleh*," he pleaded.

"I told you not to wake her up," Genia scolded. "Now she's going to cry and we won't have any peace."

"Ssssh, Zosha," Heniek said gently, puckering his lips as if he were mirroring the baby's mouth. "Don't you know your daddy?"

"Give her to me," Genia said, reaching out.

"How's my little girl?" he asked.

He bent over to kiss the baby's cheek. "Do you know your father loves you?" His lips softly touched her face, but the bristles of his beard cut her like a thousand splinters of glass. The baby shrieked with pain.

"Stop crying," he begged. "Zoshka, don't you know me?"

Genia screamed in horror. "What are you doing to her?"

"I won't hurt you," he whispered helplessly. "Please. Do you hear? All she ever does is cry when I try to play with her. For God's sake, Genia, stop her from crying!"

Her face was hot with tears. Genia rocked the baby in her arms. "All right, my love. Momma won't let anything hurt her baby."

Genia watched as Heniek read the letter, eyes ripping across the page, tripping on an English phrase, brows crushing each other, continuing. They drank tea from the white Rosenthal cups.

He folded the letter, placing it on the table.

"So it's good, Heniek. No? America!" Pronounced like notes of a musical scale.

He leaned back in the chair, sighing loudly. "*Boje, Boje.*" God, God. He repeated the word. "*Boje!*"

"America, Heniek. Finally we can go. Isn't it great news?"

He looked at her as at a child, nodding to placate her.

"It's what we've wanted," she insisted. "Aren't you happy?"

His voice was grave. "I have to make some money."

"But we have what we saved. Not much, but a little."

The chair swung back to an upright position, his shoes striking the floor. "What do you know? *Gelt.* We need *gelt.*"

"What about—" she began gingerly, trying not to make him angry. "What we've saved? Powdered eggs and milk, not using all the meat coupons—"

"*Bupkes!*" He blew up, as she feared he would, as he always did. "Not enough to buy a cup of coffee in your America!"

"What are you talking about? I thought that—"

"That what? You thought we're millionaires like your father?"

"He wasn't a million—" She protested, but does he hear?

"There's not enough. Do you understand?" he raged. "I have to make more money. Do you understand?" He opened his hand and stared into the palm.

"There's work in America," she assured him.

He turned to her. "The Jewish agencies put you up for a few months and then if you don't have a job, you starve. And don't think it is so easy to get a job. I have to do something."

"Uncle Lolek could help—"

"I don't need your family."

As she poured water into their cups, she suggested, "Maybe I could work."

"You?" He laughed. "You can't do nothing."

"I can sew."

He looked at her indulgently. "I'll take care of it."

"Not dangerous, Heniek." She approached behind his chair, wrapping her arms around his neck. "You know how nervous I get, that I can't sleep . . . "

Rancor spent, Heniek's face was boyish, gentle as a glove. He stood up, pushing the chair to the side. Moving behind her, he embraced her waist, his hands moving over the splendid roundness of her hips.

"What time of the month is it?"

Her neck flushed with blood, a red continent rising to her cheeks. "Oh, Heniek! Now? The pot—"

He took her hand, which was full of soapsuds.

/　/　/

The baby awakes to noises. The room nearly dark. A big black shape, huge and monstrous. The blanket flies away. Momma! A man's back, white, glowing, rises up over her. Daddy! Momma is reaching out to him. "America!" she cries.

"PASKUDNYAK"

Paskudnyak: From Polish/Ukranian, a man or woman who is nasty, mean, odious, contemptible, rotten, vulgar, insensitive, and dirty.

We live in Brooklyn, America. 24 Park Place. Crowned Heights. That's what I was supposed to tell a person if I got lost. My mother worried about losing me like a loose button on her blue cardigan sweater.

Our building was a dark tenement with a bomb shelter and the sign NO LOITERING, NO SPITTING, NO PLAYING BALL. From early morning until it got dark, the big children played Chinese handball against the wall while we chased each other in and out of alleyways. Everyone talked about the Dodgers. The Franklin Avenue shuttle thundered above us.

My father worked in a knitting mill in another state, New Jersey. His fellow workers on the machines, beer-drinking Americans, spoke neither Polish, Yiddish, German, nor even Russian, all of which he knew, so he had to learn English. In his freshly laundered T-shirt, all could see the blue numbers B48356 swell on the inside of his forearm as Heniek forced a loose bolt into the scalding maw.

All day, Genia's silver needle imposed order, repaired broken seams, worn elbows and knees, created lively imitations of what she saw in shop windows. *"Hello, young lover, whoever you are . . . "* She sang Hit Parade tunes as she sewed. *"Shrink boats are a-coming. . . "*

A neighbor, Mrs. Pellini, often dropped in for a cup of instant coffee. "Can you please to let out a little at the waist—God save me. I eat too much!—raise the hem, move over the buttons." My mother called it her pin money and hid the dollars in her private drawer, where she kept her cultured pearls and her father's cigarette case. Whenever Heniek objected to something she bought, Genia raised the specter of her pin money. He responded that she couldn't ride the subway with what she earned.

In the spring, she sewed matching cotton dresses for us. *Truskawki*, strawberries printed on a white background, the sleeves and waist finished with red velvet piping. As we modeled before the full-length mirror on the closet door, she cried in delight, "Look, Zosha, we're exactly the same." On a Sunday afternoon when the sun lit even our street in the subway's shadow, we wore our identical dresses to the Botanical Gardens. My father took pictures with his Leica from Germany as mother and daughter posed like movie stars under a blossoming cherry tree.

/ / /

In lieu of living family, my parents belonged to a large network of Polish Jews. All were survivors. Their names were music notes, the ladies of the *arbeit-lager:* Lola, Stella, Minka, Ruzha, Fela, Blanca, Lusia, Manusha.

Every second Wednesday, they played canasta in our living room. As they tossed bright plastic chips and picked up cards, blue numbers flashing on the insides of their arms, the stories multiplied.

"Pish, posh. I knew Mushka in the camp when she wasn't such a fancy lady. She cleaned toilets with the rest of us."

"If Bolek hadn't given me his piece of bread, I wouldn't be here. Lucky me, I was dealt two red threes!"

I understood Polish, so none of it escaped me as I played with my mother's box of buttons under the mahogany coffee table. It had books about the Warsaw Ghetto uprising and Auschwitz with photographs of concentration camp survivors in torn shifts, shaven heads—amidst bowls of celery stalks, cream cheese with scallions and radishes, Ritz crackers.

"I wouldn't give Uzek a broken cent. Now he's an important man in B'nai B'rith. During the war, he had a big mouth."

The delivery was offhand. Lineups, beatings, starvation discussed as casually as yesterday's weather. Their voices rose with excitement as they regaled one another with tales of daredevil escapes, morsels of wartime gossip, teasing each other's memories as at a college reunion. After all, most of them had been in their teens when the war broke out.

"You remember Yola? She was the not-bad-looking one with crooked teeth, who went with the German. He gave her crabs."

/ / /

When I was in second grade, we left behind the concrete shadow of the Franklin Avenue shuttle and moved uptown to the Heights. Washington Heights, that is, above Harlem and below Dyckman. Across the Hudson at Palisades Amusement Park in New Jersey, a neon roller coaster flamed, and looming larger than God was the George Washington Bridge.

"The Riviera" was carved in stone over the entrance to our apartment building. On either side of the marble columns were curse words in black spray paint.

Our third-floor apartment overlooked 161st Street. When I wasn't out, leaning on parked cars, passing a single Salem among giggly teenage girls, I sat on the fire escape of my parents' pink bedroom. I watched my street for hours: boys pitched broomstick baseball, slithering on their stomachs to plunk wax-melted bottle-caps into skully boxes. Nearby, completely ignoring them, girls hopped between chalked potsy boxes, bounced pink balls through all the letters of the alphabet, jumped double Dutch without getting tangled in the two ropes, flying from side to side. Children whizzed past on tricycles as bent-over old ladies crawled up the block, pushing shopping carts of groceries. In the afternoon's fading sunlight, mothers wheeled black-hooded baby carriages.

As I sat on the fire escape, pigeons pecked at my lunch, an egg salad sandwich, which I had refused to eat the day before. The white bread was moist and pulpy. "I'm not throwing away food that could save someone's life," Genia insisted, placing it next to me on the windowsill. "If I have to, I'll give it to you every day of your life. You can't have anything until you eat your sandwich."

I crumbled pieces of the crust and tossed them to a fat gray pigeon who snatched them in his beak. We were both content. What my mother didn't know was that I had discovered Chico's miraculous French fries across the street from school. When you stuck your hand in the brown paperbag, the grease and ketchup flavored your fingers, which you could lick, and the taste lasted all day. It cost fifteen cents for regular, and a quarter for large. I rarely had enough money to buy, but I took dibs on my friends' fries.

The Heights made Brooklyn—mostly Italian, Irish, and Jewish—seem tame. Especially the streets east of Broadway. We rode the uptown AA past 116th Street, 125th, to 161st, our station, a dark, piss-scented grotto littered with broken bottles of Thunderbird. When you got to the street, St. Nicholas, you had to walk fast without seeming scared. Men lurked in parked cars, in doorways, hanging out of windows with their pants open. They exposed themselves, jerked off in front of you, followed you for blocks breathing heavily, whispering things in a voice that got inside of you, creeping into your sleep: *mi puta, te amo* . . . I never told my parents. They had to know, I figured, or they didn't want to know.

The High Holidays descended upon us. It began with Rosh Hashanah. My father poured red wine into the engraved silver goblets from his family's home. He had dug them up after the war. Now he stood at the head of the table, mumbling in Hebrew as he held the goblet his father had once held.

"Heniek," Genia said, sitting down at the table. "Enough already. We're hungry and you're still *dovening*."

"Quiet!" he said sharply. "No wonder Zosha doesn't know nothing. There's no respect."

Then came Yom Kippur, the Day of Repentence. The only time of the year I didn't have to eat. I wasn't even supposed to brush my teeth.

They lit *yortzeit* candles. Here," my father said, passing me the prayer book opened to *Zikhronot*. Remembrances.

He pointed to a passage. "Read this in English." *May we never abandon our memories. May our memories inspire deeds which lead us to life and love, to blessings and peace.*

I looked at my parents. Their memories did not lead them to peace, only tearful retelling of loss. In fact, they did nothing but remember. My mother pacing from room to room in the apartment, weeping inconsolably. When I wanted to go outside, she turned on me. *"Paskudnyak!* It's the day I lost my whole family."

After months of gaga adoration, I finally succeeded in becoming one of the Cleopatras. They were a tough, cigarette-smoking clique of girls who rushed home after school to worship at the shrine of "American Bandstand," then slithered through the streets in teased-out hairdos with satin bows clipped above the bangs, Liz Taylor makeup, and the cheapest, tackiest gear this side of Frederick's of Hollywood. Felicidad flashed black see-through tops, her major bosom popping out of a black lace push-up bra. Cookie was a color freak; this week's special, purple: purple sweater, skirt, tights, shoes, and headband. Lola's glittering turquoise eyeliner started at her lobes and stopped at the bridge of her nose. I wore a tight black skirt, off-black runny stockings, and white lipstick, but my claim to fame was my hair. When fully teased and sprayed, it measured four and a half inches high.

Wherever the Cleopatras went, acne-ridden boys with greasy pompadours followed, buzzing around us. Their transistors wailed, "When a man loves a woman . . . " as they flicked Duncan yo-yos at each other, cut loud farts, made gross remarks, and ran after us, attacking with water balloons and pea shooters.

Usually Felicidad and Cookie made out with Hector and Jesus, but sometimes they switched. I had a secret crush on Carlos, Jesus' brother, who was a dead ringer for George Chakiris in *West Side Story*. We exchanged furtive, burning glances, consummated at Cookie's party where we had French-kissed during Seven Minutes of Heaven.

At sunset, the Cleopatras met on 158th Street, across the street from Mt. Sinai *shul*. We smoked Salems, teased our hair higher, and sprayed it as the Jews prayed at the evening Sabbath service.

My father looked up from his *New York Times*. We rarely encountered each other. During the week, he left for work while I was at school and returned after midnight. Most Saturdays he worked, but not today. "Where are you going?" he demanded.

"Out," I said.

"You look like a tramp," he said, inspecting me.

Transistor radio plugged to my ear, I lip-synched "My boyfriend's back and there's gonna be trouble," having gotten myself semi-dolled up in Pink Passion lipstick, a chartreuse satin blouse, tight black skirt with a slit on the side, off-black stockings, and roach-killer boots.

"Everyone dresses like this," I told him. Then figuring I'd be clever, I added, "Dad, this is the style in America."

"Who cares about style? Genia!" he called. "You let her leave the house like this?"

My mother rushed out of the kitchen, wiping her hands on the dishtowel tied around her waist. "What do you want me to do?" she demanded. "Lock her up?"

"You should do something before she gets locked up by the police. A Jewish girl walking on the street like that," he grumbled, picking up the newspaper, which had fanned at his feet.

I put my hand out, saying softly, "Mom, I need my allowance."

"Talk to your father," she said, returning to the kitchen.

"Dad." I approached slowly. "Can I have two dollars and fifty cents, please? Cookie and Lola and me are going to the movies."

Without looking up, he said, "Tramps. Streetwalkers. Not companions for you. Why don't you wash that crap off your face."

The downstairs buzzer would sound in five minutes.

He sat there in his dictator pose.

"Please," I insisted. "You owe me my allowance."

"Give me peace!" he cried. "You won't get a penny until you wash your face. Look at you."

"What's wrong with the way I look?"

For a moment, our eyes met. Then he turned back to his paper. "I don't trust you," he said.

The downstairs bell buzzed three times. I buzzed back, knowing that my friends would wait five minutes, then leave.

"Please, Dad."

"Leave me alone!" he cried out. Then suddenly, he was screaming. "I survived for this? To see my own daughter turn into filth? I should have died in the camps."

"It's my allowance, Dad," I screamed back. "You owe me it!"

His newspaper did not stir as they gathered at the wall on Riverside Drive without me, feet swinging as they slapped each other five, strutting their stuff to 181st Street where they headed for the balcony smoking section of the RKO Coliseum. My father was immovable.

Finally, overcome by tears, I gave up. As I walked to my room, I heard a cheerless laugh. "Zosha, come here," he called me.

I turned to face my father. Two dollars dangled from his fingers. "Here, *paskudnyak*," he said.

As I tried to grab the bills, his hand withdrew. He repeated this trick. It amused him to watch his daughter leaping up and down like a seal.

"What do you have to cry about?" he mocked. "I never had nothing, not even before the war." He handed me two dollars. "Go to the stinking movies."

Running up the stairs, toes numb from my roach-killer boots, I found Cookie and Lola in the back row of the RKO balcony. They weren't alone. This guy with a toppling pompadour had his arm around Lola. Both smoked cigarettes. On the screen, Natalie Wood and Steve McQueen were making out in *Love with the Proper Stranger*. So were Cookie and Jesus. And sitting next to Jesus—I couldn't believe it—his gorgeous brother, Carlos.

I, of course, sat down at the other end of the row. It was the only cool thing to do. Cookie beckoned me. "Hey, yo!" But I shook my head and watched what happened when Natalie Wood went all the way.

I felt the heat of his presence before I turned. Carlos

had slipped in next to me, his arm tactfully draping my seat. "Hi," he whispered in my ear. "How you doin'?"

"Fine."

Those were the only words exchanged. As we watched Natalie Wood discover she was in trouble, Carlos's arm moved stealthily from the seat, grazing my shoulder, to firmly surround me. Soon his lips were teasing mine. I couldn't resist. I wanted his lips against mine and then his tongue. I kissed him as hard as I could, thinking of how much I hated my father.

We kept kissing, but he moved closer, holding me tighter, rubbing his knee softly against my thighs. I felt breathless. Meanwhile, Steve McQueen took Natalie Wood to get the "operation."

"How you doin'?" he whispered.

"Fine," I answered, my voice quaking. "You?"

We just kept kissing, my lips bruising, but I didn't care as he hugged me harder, rubbing his knee between my legs. I clutched his arms, pushing against him. I felt hot, my cheeks flushed, out of breath. Suddenly, I was panting like I might hyperventilate. Was this an orgasm? It was so different from when I did it alone.

We were slipping out of our seats. I threw myself against his hipbone, his leg. More. "Oh, Carlos," I sighed, trying to muffle my breathing. But he was panting too, pressing against me, grinding against my hip.

"*Mi caracita.*"

Suddenly, the flash of a light beamed on our faces. "What are you doing?" an outraged voice demanded.

We pulled ourselves up to a sitting position, trying hastily to straighten out our clothes. "Nothing," said Carlos, tucking in his shirt.

"We won't have this," declared the middle-aged black

woman in a navy bellhop suit. Her flashlight formed a yellow triangle around us. "You must leave."

"We paid our money," Carlos said.

"You leave right now or I'll call the guard," she threatened.

"Fuck you and your family," Jesus called out.

"Punks," the usher muttered, walking back up the aisle.

"Yo, Carlos!" Jesus called from across the row. "What's happen?"

"It's cool, man."

"Hey, spic and span," an angry voice shouted, "Shut the fuck up!"

"Your mother!" another voice called.

As Natalie Wood wept desperate tears because she was in love with Steve McQueen but he would never respect her since she'd gotten pregnant when she went all the way with him, we felt the clamp of strong fingers on our shoulders. Carlos and I were ushered out of the theater by a short guy with incredibly muscular arms. "I'm calling your parents, you hoodlums."

"I don't know what you do, who you're with," Genia said as we rode the bus to Yeshiva Rabbi Soleveichik on 185th Street, where my father insisted she enroll me. "It's better here. You'll be with Jewish children, not the *goyim* on the street."

But I despised Judaism. Lighting candles to remember the dead. Holidays and high holidays, which introduced yet more taboos. Why did they talk about *shvartzes* as if they were subhumans? As if Jews were a different race and we mustn't consort with anyone else.

My mother's inconsistent rites of observation! Bacon and ham were okay, but no pork chops. Spareribs from the Chinese restaurant were okay too. The two-faced double standards for inside and outside the house. Every Saturday, my mother turned on the radio to listen to the "Make-Believe Ballroom," watched the "Million Dollar Movie," and so did I. But if I was going outside, I had to observe Shabbos and not wear pants.

"You must look decent. They tried to destroy us," she told me. "Now we must show how well we dress."

For my interview with the rabbi, my teased hairdo was forcibly reduced by fifty percent. My mother made me wear my blue pleated skirt with a white ruffled blouse—Israel's colors, she reminded me. But I sported my black leather roach-killer boots. I was a slum goddess, after all.

Inside the red brick building, all the boys wore *yarmulkes.* As they raced through the halls, their arms filled with books, the strings of their *tzitzit* streamed behind them like leashes. The girls walked quietly. Upon noticing me, they began to whisper among themselves. One boy grunted loudly, "Ugh." As I seemed to scratch my head, I gave them all a subtle middle finger.

In the elevator, my mother raised her slip. She then pulled down the hem of her blue wool dress. "All right?" she asked, turning around. "I copied this pattern from Vogue."

We entered a musty-smelling office, papers strewn over the old, scratched-up desk and on the chair, leather-bound volumes from ceiling to floor. As the rabbi looked up from the text on his desk, I could see his long, white beard, white *peyes,* and sharp blue eyes.

He opened a book with large Hebrew letters. "Will you read these?" he said, pointing with his finger.

"I don't know how," I said, staring down blankly while of course recognizing the *aleph, bet, gimel, dalet, hay . . .*

"Haven't your parents sent you to Hebrew school?" the rabbi inquired.

I nodded. Our text, *The History of the Jewish People,* started with Abraham and Moses, through Disraeli, to Ben Gurion, Leonard Bernstein, and Bernie Schwartz, known to his fans as Tony Curtis. The teacher was a balding, dogmatic man who despised questions, especially from girls. A crocheted *yarmulke* with a black circle in its center was bobby-pinned to his short hair. When he turned around to write on the blackboard, I imagined shooting a rubber band and paper clip. Bull's-eye!

"Young lady," the rabbi demanded, "Don't make me angry. What's the first letter of the Hebrew alphabet?"

"*Aleph.*" I nearly spat the word.

His blue eyes observed me from their pink pockets. "You don't want to go to yeshiva? Why? Don't you want an education?"

Yeshiva meant four hours of religion in addition to regular school. I crossed my arms. "I'm an atheist," I said, having come across the word in *The Fountainhead* by Ayn Rand.

"Don't be rude," my mother misunderstood. "She doesn't mean that," she apologized, cuffing me on the back of my neck.

The rabbi studied me, shaking his head. "You speak because you don't know. Is that what you want? To be stupid like the rest of the world?"

"I don't want to go to yeshiva," I declared, wondering why Jews always thought they were so smart.

"Do you think you'd be happier going to public school?" he asked.

I nodded.

"You know there won't be many white children," he said.

"I don't care," I said.

"You like the colored?" my mother asked. "When they beat you up, you weren't so happy."

In sixth grade, a group of older girls followed me after school. "Balloonhead!" they called. "Shake it, don't break it, took your momma nine months to make it." Their taunts grew louder. "She thinks she's hot." I walked fast, knowing Broadway wasn't far. They followed on my heels. "Hey, girl," someone called, "when I talk to you, you listen." I started to run. Suddenly, a girl grabbed my arms from behind and threw me down. I landed on my knees, the concrete ripping my stockings. My knees bled as I made my way home. My mother had found my bloody stockings in the garbage.

"Have you no shame?" the rabbi demanded suddenly.

I stared at the ground to keep from meeting his stinging blue eyes.

"After what your parents went through," he said.

I crossed my arms, not answering him.

"Say something!" my mother urged. "What's wrong with you?"

I shifted my weight to the other foot.

"We can't force you to learn." The rabbi shrugged. "She doesn't belong here, Mrs. Palovsky."

My mother nodded. "I didn't think so. It was my husband's idea. In Poland, his family was very religious."

The rabbi was through with us, but Genia continued. "My family was assimilated. Still they took us away and murdered everyone."

"We must honor the memory of those who perished," the rabbi said, standing up slowly. His dark jacket was stained. "May everything work out for the best, God willing."

"Are you happy now?" she asked as we walked out of the building. "Now you can rot on the street with your juvenile delinquent friends."

"They're not juvenile delinquents," I insisted. "They just like to dress tough."

"But Zosha, you belong with these people? Their families drink and the husbands beat up the wives. *Paskudnyak!* Why can't you be normal—like Daddy and me?"

REMEMBER 6,000,000

"Oh, no," I groaned, glancing at the clock. Eleven-fifteen. "I never sleep this late!"

"Sunday morning," Ludwig yawned, stretching his long arms. "C'm'ere." He pulled me to his chest.

"Uh-uh." I disentangled myself. "I've got to be on the East Side at noon."

He looked blankly at me.

"Yom Hashoah," I said, beginning to open and shut drawers. "Remember? I told you?"

"Oh," he said, then grimaced, "right."

I looked down at Lud, my gentle gentile, my beautiful *sheygetz,* who lay on his back with his eyes shut. His hair, coltish brown, was profoundly straight. God didn't have such straight hair. Another species from mine, dark and serpentine. And his skin, white, opalescent, nearly hairless except for the deep brown forest between his legs and a flowering around his collarbone that he called his third armpit. With his long brown hair, full mustache, and beard, he looked like young Jesus.

I reached inside the closet, pulling out a hanger from way in the back. A blue-gray dress. As I slipped it on, I called to Lud. "Hey, open your eyes. What do you think?"

"It matches your eyes," my mother had said, handing me the dress some months ago. "I sewed it from a Vogue pattern. Very stylish." I had never worn it.

"Nice." Ludwig sat up. "I'd go with you," he said in his slightly German-accented English. "Except I don't think anyone at the temple would be too happy to see me." He cocked his head, grinning.

I tried to imagine the scene. "I think you're right."

"Let me help you with the zipper."

I sat down on the bed. "God, I don't want to go."

The enormity of the event was hitting me like a bad trip. I had somehow forgotten, had hardly even thought of Yom Hashoah over the weekend. Talk about avoidance.

"Then don't," Lud said softly.

"As if I have a choice."

"There's always a choice, Zosha." Hand on my spine, he drew me to him.

"Yeah?" I resisted. Didn't he know my family? A year ago, I had brought Ludwig to meet my parents. We had been seeing each other for eight months.

After beef flanken and *galuskas*, potato dumplings, which Lud said were better than his own mother's, over my mother's cheese babka and tea, we told them we were engaged.

"I love your daughter very much," Lud added, squeezing my hand.

My father sipped his tea. Then said, "Your people loved us so much that they pointed the way for the Gestapo."

"Lud didn't do anything!" I responded.

My father turned to me. "What do you know? They would sooner kill us than cross the street."

Lud had stood up. "You don't have to say anymore."

"What about his family?" my father's voice grew louder. "Do you know where they were during the war?"

"Maybe if he converted to Judaism?" my mother mused doubtfully.

"Are you circumcised?" my father demanded.

"Dad!"

"Of course not."

"You must be circumcised," my mother said.

"Never."

"We have nothing to say."

"I love him," I said.

"I don't want you in our house."

"Stop it, Dad!" I screamed.

"Are you staying?" Lud demanded.

I had looked from his burning eyes to my parents. As I stood between them, the walls of my family's home narrowed. I was in love and wanted to join Lud to live in the larger world outside.

"I'll be right back," I had told him. I packed an extra pair of jeans, a sweater, some T-shirts, and my good underwear in a knapsack.

My parents were in the kitchen. We could hear the water running. "I'm leaving," I had called.

My mother rushed out, wiping her hands on her apron. "Zosha," she cried. "You're wrong to do this. Your father didn't mean—"

"I have a mouth. You don't have to speak for me." He stood behind her.

"Dad—" I began.

"If you leave," he said slowly, "I won't have you back."

"Heniek, she's your daughter!"

"Are you ready?" Lud asked me softly. "You don't have to do this."

"I'm going," I said, my voice shattering.

"Zosha!" my mother cried out.

"I don't know her." My father turned his back to me. "My daughter is dead."

Now I held on to Lud tightly, as if I might fall off some precipice. He cupped my breast in his hand, kissing it. I closed my eyes. We had both been born on the other side, in Europe, after the war, to scarred survivors. We shared wounds the way addicts shared needles.

Lud's father, a Russian soldier, had not returned from the war. The story was that his mother had walked from Russia to Germany with her two young sons, Ludwig and his brother, Heine. They were *Volksdeutsch,* whatever that was. Eventually, they ended up in Livingston, New Jersey. When Heine grew up, he returned to Germany, dying soon afterward from eating poisonous mushrooms.

There was something else too. Ludwig had told me on our first night together.

"I was fourteen, going through puberty. No father, etc. My mother and I lived in the upstairs of a house we shared with the town judge, if you can believe it. Anyway," he had continued, "what I want to tell you about might make you walk out the door."

My stomach had gnarled in anticipation. What could be so awful?

"At that time, I was very interested in guns. I began to collect them. Also memorabilia from World War Two. I was always fascinated—you could say obsessed with the war."

"Me too," I said. "I understand."

"I know that you understand," he said, looking into my eyes.

"Most Americans have no idea."

"Zoe, the story is that someone found out about the guns. They broke into our attic. They saw my collection. The fact that the judge lived downstairs turned it into a major scandal."

"What happened?"

He had opened the drawer of a desk, taking out a photo album. Turned to a yellowed article. The *Livingston Courier*. May 1962. "NEO-NAZI FOUND WITH ARSENAL."

"Gosh," I had said stupidly, trying to take it in. *Neo-Nazi!* Ludwig?

". . . A search of the attic revealed two rifles, a compressed air pistol, two sling shots, several knives and ammunition, as well as an old German war flag, newspapers from the Nazi era and a school notebook with the letters 'SS' written on it, the initials of the elite Nazi units responsible for wartime atrocities."

I had placed the album down with a thud. "I can't look at this."

"I was fourteen," Lud said. "And very confused."

"Why'd you show me?"

"So you'd know. It ended there, Zoe. I swear. But I don't want to have secrets from you. I respect you. I respect your parents' experience. I don't want to give anyone pain."

He was my Nazi. I loved him with a wild passion. I stared

at him continually. I stared through him but could only see shadows. I never had any idea what he was thinking.

"You're a big girl," Ludwig insisted now, as I was about to leave. "You don't have to do anything you don't want to."

"Sure," I said bravely, grabbing my keys off a hook near the door.

"I'll pick up some Chinese for later," he called after me.

In 1951, the Israeli Knesset proclaimed Yom Hashoah, the Day of Remembrance for the Martyrs and Heroes of the Holocaust. It came once a year, but I didn't need a holiday. I remembered the Holocaust every day of my life. *Never forget.* That was my tattoo. Never forget.

As I walked across Central Park, I dug into my pocketbook, finding a silver case with a mother-of-pearl cover. It had been my mother's father's cigarette case. I snapped it open, removing a joint rolled thin. Ah, holy weed.

I lit up, inhaling its delicious bouquet. This was my medicine. This was my religion. Slowly, I felt an opening of the gates. I could breathe. A peaceful calm descended on me as I walked past the pond. The trees revealed tiny red buds. I stopped to watch ducks competing with pigeons for bread crusts on the ground, thrown by a gleeful old lady in a gray bathrobe. I felt connected to them all.

I recalled a time when Ludwig and I had walked through the park. Winter was at its most bitter. As we strolled past chess players, the sun on our faces, we kissed.

Suddenly a tiny, gnomish man appeared next to us. He wore a plaid hat with a feather, just like my father's. I knew it wasn't my imagination. The man was staring at us. Finally he said, "You're a Jewish girl, no?"

"What?" I asked.

"Jewish. You're Jewish," he had insisted.

I held on more tightly to Ludwig's arm.

"What business do you have with him?" he demanded, pointing at Lud.

"Let's go," I said.

"What do you mean?" Ludwig asked.

"A Jewish girl shouldn't be with one of them. It's not right."

I had pulled Lud's arm. "Come on!" I urged. "I'm leaving."

The man followed us for several more steps. "You shouldn't be together," he declared. "Go to your home, daughter of Israel."

At home, Ludwig quietly filled his meerschaum pipe with Balkan Sobranie tobacco. He never said much anyway. I stared at him. He was so beautiful, so poetically deep to me. But what was he thinking? I loved him with a still-greater passion.

When the apple blossoms flowered, pink petals dusting the concrete, Lud gave me an antique gold ring with a jade stone surrounded by four tiny rubies. I wore it on my fourth finger. *NEO-NAZI TO MARRY HOLOCAUST SURVIVORS' DAUGHTER.*

Day of Remembrance of the Holocaust. I said the words like a mantra to myself. Remember what? Six million, of course. That strangely rounded-off number. A downtown artist had painted six million red marks on scraps of wood, on tools and surfaces of chairs and tables. The number of dots was unfathomable. He called it *Six Million Marks.*

Remember. Made up of the Latin *re*, 'back,' 'again' and *memorare,* 'mindful.' Mind full of what? The heaviest, densest guilt trip in the galaxy. Was *this* survivor guilt?

That's what good Dr. Lipschitz told me. A solid classification. Survivor's guilt. How could I have survivor guilt if I wasn't a survivor? I was born five years after the war had ended. And yet. In my deepest, most involuntary place, my stomach, I carried the Holocaust. I had all the moves. I was born with the stealth, with the terrors.

Remember. There were times I forgot. Oh, shame. During sex, when the mind became completely body, animal, instinct. Dope gave me moments too. When I could hear other music in my head besides the mean finger-pointing, blaming, ridiculing, insulting voice.

Remember the dead. But I had never known any of them. Even their names were dead. As if they'd never existed. I pretended I was born like Venus on a seashell. Without a past. Without history.

I could hear the words of the Baal Shem Tov: "Forgetfulness leads to exile. Remembrance is the secret of redemption."

Oh, gentle oblivion. I inhaled deeply. I imagined the smoke creating a bulletproof shield around me. It kept away demons, Nazis, the hater inside of me, protecting me as I walked toward the maw of the monster.

I snuffed my joint as I reached Fifth Avenue, returning the silver case to my pocketbook. I came out of the park at Seventy-second Street. I knew Temple Emanu-El had to be nearby. What was the cross street? In this nightmare, I walked up and down the most elegant avenue in the world, staring up at the white stone buildings, burgundy-uniformed doormen protecting their portals of privilege.

I must find my way. I was probably standing right in

front of Temple Emanu-El. Surely it was a grand structure. But where the hell was it?

Finally, I approached an Orthodox-looking Jewish woman, wearing a fetching *frum* hat, with three children, and pushing an umbrella stroller with an infant.

She was hardly older than I was. A baby machine. A Jewish baby maker who produced only girls. But maybe one could draw a Talmud scholar who worked in the Diamond District on Forty-seventh Street. "Excuse me," I said, "Do you know where Temple Emanu-El—?"

"It's further south," she cut me off. "I don't really know."

It occurred to me that Temple Emanu-El, mecca of Reform Judaism, must be anathema to her. A dark-haired little girl with large, blue eyes stared out at me.

An American flag flew at full mast at the entrance to Temple Emanu-El. I stood before it, startled by the immensity and grandeur. The most un-Jewish structure one could imagine, except for its modest Star of David within an immense circle of latticework.

I thought we were supposed to be people of the invisible god, I protested silently, who shunned ostentation. Not the *yekkers*, as German Jews were called, yukking it up with their red carpets and cushioned seats where men sat with women. Few wore *yarmulkes*, a *shtetl* remnant. This was wealthy, privileged Jewry, mostly pre-war arrivals whose refugee past had long been eclipsed by business and professional status.

For the Day of Remembrance, they opened their doors to the noisy, pushy DPs and greenhorns from uptown and the boroughs, like my mother in her dark coat with the fox collar. If they bought tickets, of course. These were successful Jews who lived on the East Side—that is, the

Upper East Side, attended Metropolitan Museum openings and Sotheby's, demanded private day schools for their children, who had complete sets of the *Encyclopedia Britannica*. They were fervently, culturally Jewish. Every week's mail brought the brown sleeve of *The New Yorker*.

A man handed me an offset program as I entered. "LET US REMEMBER THOSE WHO PERISHED IN THE NAZI HOLOCAUST," it proclaimed. "JOIN US IN PAYING TRIBUTE TO THE SIX MILLION JEWISH MARTYRS. WE WLL NOT FORGET, WE WILL NOT FORGIVE. WE REMEMBER."

I walked into Temple Emanu-El stoned, fucked up, half-fearing the spectacle of skeletal figures in torn blue and white shifts. Instead, I saw the well-fed survivors wrapped in fur coats and Florida tans, seemingly well-healed Jews who had their society and ceremonies, chattering excitedly in the aisles. "Oh, there's Lola Rosenberg with her new husband . . . Look how handsome is Mayor Lindsay!"

In my worst moments, I hated the victims. They deserved it. If they'd been cleverer, stronger, less greedy, they wouldn't have been stuck in Europe in the first place. Look at all the emigrés. Einstein, Mann, Brecht. I hated the weakness and stupidity of the victims. Why couldn't they have gotten out? Somehow. Like the rich German Jews, who brought over mahogany breakfronts and candelabras.

"I'm not the first generation," a voice behind me boasted. "I'm the very first generation!" The highly rouged woman wore a navy silk suit with a black-and-white sticker on her lapel: REMEMBER 6,000,000.

Remember what? Parents with no parents? Uncles, aunts, cousins who are only names, and they are forgotten too? Remember to hate? Whom? Germans? Poles? Arabs?

The voice grew furious. It always happened.

To remember that we are hated, wanted dead? Were these our heirlooms? A large-scale model of Auschwitz, the slogan Arbeit Macht Frei arched over the gate.

One of my mother's friends, Bella Gold, trapped me as I tried to be inconspicuous, walking down a side aisle of the temple. She had teased blond hair with wings. "Your mother made for you that dress? Very nice. Your parents are sitting on the other side," she said, pointing. "It's so good that you came. We need the Second Generation to know."

I tried to free myself.

"My Hela isn't interested," she continued tragically. "Today she goes to a stupid baseball game with her boyfriend. On Yom Hashoah. Have you ever heard such a thing?"

I recalled that it was Hela who had coined the term "Lodz beige" to describe the strange color, never seen in nature, that transformed these women from Holocaust brunettes to Hollywood blonds.

Suddenly a nervous hush filled the sanctuary. The spotlight caught the dark, hollowed sockets of his eyes, the thin wisps of hair, a deeply lined face and gaunt body. Elie Wiesel.

Once, the *New York Times* had published a photograph of his Buchenwald barracks with a dozen blank-eyed skulls, a white circle drawn around his recognizable face. His number A-7713.

"Let us tell tales . . ." he began softly. Temple Emanu-El reverberated with his chilling voice. I closed my eyes. All I could hear were the words, spinning in a turbid soup of suffering. SURVIVOR REMEMBER THE UNSPEAKABLE NIGHT DARKNESS GOD SIX MILLION DEATH NIGHTMARES

FORSAKEN SILENCE TO BEAR WITNESS LEGACY NOT FOR-
GET SURVIVOR.

Survivor. Once we were DPs, despised by others, including American Jews. Certainly my parents thought of themselves as victims. I was the child of victims. The ones bullied in the schoolyard, decimated by pogroms, and then the Final Solution. They didn't get out soon enough, when they still could. I never understood why a single sibling, aunt, or uncle in either of my parents' families hadn't packed up and left on the first train out of Poland.

"Tata wanted to go, but my mother said no. 'What will we do with the furniture? We can't just leave *everything*,'" my mother told me. "Now I spit on things. We lost every-thing anyway."

"Where would we go?" my father responded when I asked him. "You think in Germany it was better? Austria? Hungary? There was nowhere to go."

"How about Russia?" I asked him.

"There were people who walked to Russia," he answered. "It's true. I know someone." He shrugged. "Do you how many generations we lived in Lodz? We knew no one, we had no place to go."

Some years later, history was rewritten, my parents anointed as survivors. Their perception of themselves as victims shifted, and they began to think of themselves with a new-found pride. But it seemed such a fiction to me. Now people admired my parents, and even me by association. Because I had parents who had survived concentration camps and I was Second Generation, capitalized like the word Holocaust. "We're honored to have you in our home," the host said, his eyes moist as he took my coat.

I sometimes questioned whether Heniek and Genia had truly survived—their youth, innocence, trust in the world, belief in humanity—*pouf*—extinguished like a light. I had inherited their original, deep sense of injury. I was still a child of victims.

The memorial candle-lighting was about to begin. The women in black huddled near the altar. Long white tapers lit up faces that were now deeply wrinkled.

The line began to move. My mother rose up the steps gravely. She floated across the stage in her good black dress with pearl buttons. Her black lace veil fluttered as she lit a candle for the Czestochowa dead.

Our eyes met for moment. I could see her tears. She was still the white-scarved beauty chosen from the Selection line to live, though her kerchief was black lace. My chest felt tight.

Afterward, she had joined my father. As I approached, she stared up at me. "I'm so glad you're here." She hugged me.

I turned away from my mother's moist green eyes, which threatened to drown me.

Her voice was near worshipful. "I knew you would look beautiful in the dress," she whispered.

I slipped into their row, taking a seat between them. "Zosha," my mother sighed. Her mother's name.

My father acknowledged me with a brisk nod, then turned his attention to the service.

The yeshiva day school children, dressed in white shirts, navy blue skirts, and pants, marched to the center. They began to sing. "*Shtiller, shtiller*—softer, softer, let's be silent, graves are growing here . . . "

I thought about how graves were marked not only to sanctify the plot of the dead but also to differentiate it from the land of the living. I sat there, sandwiched between my parents.

We were there, they nodded together. *We were there.* And I wasn't. Yet as I looked from my mother to my father, I had a vision of a colossal stone statue, centuries-old. The imposing monarch, his smaller, narrow-hipped queen next to him, and, carved between them, a tiny slip of a princess.

FIRST STORY

In the beginning, there was comfort. Genia's family spent every summer in the apartment on Alleya 1 in Czestochowa with Uncle Lolek, a doctor. There was a swing in the backyard, a clothesline on which Aunt Tusha's enormous brassieres ballooned in the wind among the forsythia.

In 1938, her father's shop on Mokotowska was looted by their neighbors, who resented his brisk business in custom-made suits. A week later, before the *Aktion* that would turn Warsaw into a filthy, walled-in Jewish ghetto, they arranged their escape to Czestochowa, still safe from the Nazis.

They packed their apartment, filling five wooden chests with clothing, her father's tweed and plaid worsted fabrics from the shop, the carved headboard, a silver menorah with eight tiny lion heads, an iron pot filled with Momma's *cholent*. Before they left, Father took Genia down to the basement. Raising a wooden floorboard, he showed her where the jewelry was hidden.

Her mother had sewn *zlotys* into her coat lining. She could feel the coins rustle behind her knees as the train shook. Paper money was hidden in the rolls of her pageboy. Jesse's stuffed elephant held more dollars.

Czestochowa was a small town, known for its Black Madonna. Alleya 1 overlooked the market square. The family settled into the second floor of Uncle Lolek's house. Six months later, Selection began. Left line, right line.

Her girlfriend Ruth's family with the aging grandfather, the lame seamstress, Perla; Janusz, the butcher who couldn't breathe—to the right. Grolek Stern, her young mathematics tutor, pushed a rusty wagon with one valise tied with cord, boxes of books, and his beloved mongrel, Bog. To the left. Genia watched from the attic window as the dog was shot. Grolek had started out of the line when the policeman turned his gun on him. He bowed his head and ran back into the line.

Her mother's hair was dyed with black henna. She had rubbed her face with a beet so she blushed like a young girl, so pretty. False documents had been purchased dearly, showing that Genia had worked in an electric factory.

"But Momma, I want to go to *gymnazium*."

"*Spokojnie!* Be still!" she said sharply. "Can't you see what is happening?"

Genia began to cry. "But you said if I learned my mathematics—"

Zosia stroked her daughter's shoulders. "My radish, you'll go after the war."

The morning of Yom Kippur, the clouds burst with rain. The Mauser's butt hit the doorframe three times. Genia's family carried cartons, cans of sprats, bedding, Father's fabrics for barter. Slowly, they walked to the market square. Momma held Jesse's hand. The night before, she had made Genia wash her panties and brown wool stockings. "We don't know what will be. You must keep yourself clean, no matter what."

Momma had tied a white woolen kerchief around Genia's hair just before they left. A rough peasant weave, unfinished around the edges so it fringed, the wool made her head itch. She had tried to pull it off, but Momma insisted. "Genusha, please. It may be cold in the place we're going . . . " Her voice trailed off like smoke.

As they stood on line, Genia suddenly heard the words: "*Bialy szalik!* Where's the girl with the white kerchief?"

Genia had hidden behind her mother. The family was still together. She could see Jesse's stuffed elephant. She grabbed his other hand. Maybe the policeman wanted to steal her new fur-lined boots.

The Polish policeman found her. åShe had dropped to her knees. "You!" He commanded, pulling her by the arm. "The other line."

"Momma!" she cried, holding on to her waist. "Don't let them take me!"

The policeman, who wore tall black boots, pulled her away. "*Idz!*" he commanded. Go! Her family only several feet away. She wept, not even feeling the fingers grabbing her, scratching her hand with sharp nails, until she heard a hushed "Genia."

It was Clara! Uncle Edek's daughter, one class higher in the *gymnazium*. "Why'd they take me?" she cried. "I want to be with Momma and—"

"Stop it." Clara's eyes were savage. "Look at that line you want to go to so badly. You see the mothers with babies? The men? Either children or old. Sick ones, cripples. They say they are taking them to a larger place."

"Momma and Tata—"

"Sure." Clara spat the word. "Their grave."

"What about Jesse?" She whispered her baby brother's name.

Genia kept the white kerchief through the war. Even when it was torn like a *shmatte,* she kept it, holding it under her nose when she slept so she could smell the wool, so much like her mother's skin. She kept it until they were liberated by the Russians.

In one moment, she had a family, then she lost them all. Her whole family was taken away. *Pouf!* She never saw them again.

After Selection, Genia was sent to a labor camp in the outskirts of Czestochowa, Hasag Hugo Schneider. Month after month, she stood in an assembly line, cleaning gun shells. She was always hungry. Filthy water with turnip and potato peels, the piece of stinking bread only made it worse, but she forced it into her stomach.

Genia found a *lager* "husband," Janek, who worked in the men's section with dynamite powder, which had blinded his left eye. She lost her virginity on a typhus-infested mattress in Janek's barracks. The other men were there, their eyes open but unmoving. He said they couldn't hear even though one, Srolek, lay below them.

It was the first time for everything. No graduated fondlings: begin with breasts and if that's permitted, stomach and thighs. Each step an opening of the heart, cheeks flushed, heat pumping through the body. Hers was done and it was rudimentary. Afterward, Genia had to pee in the *pushka,* a metal can, and all could watch her squat. But no one did. Not even Janek.

In her barracks, the Polish guards tormented her. Pietruszka, with her haunches like a horse's and her fat, veined legs in black hose rolled around her ankles. She enjoyed digging her pointy, laced shoes into Genia's waist as she scrubbed under the cots. If Genia protested, there'd be more. But if she seemed to bear it with equanimity, ignore her, Pietruszka grew wrathful. So she had to strike an attitude of dumb acquiescence, as if she were a donkey.

And what of the other witch, Marchevka, named by them all Carrot, because of her hideous hair, actually the color of dried blood. She watched Genia wash the toilets, grabbing her by the hair if she was unsatisfied. It was Marchevka who gave permission to relieve themselves.

The guards were ignorant, without schooling, except for the bootcamp of their brutal imaginations. And Genia had studied Latin, knew how to conjugate verbs, repeating them to herself obsessively. *Veni, venitus.*

She had been a girl, sixteen; suddenly, she was in her twenties. When they were liberated in January 1945, she found her mother's uncle Lolek, who, as a doctor, had survived in several camps. Before, he had been a stout man who favored potato latkes with sour cream. Now he was lean as a thief, his expression furtive. He had lost his wife, Tusha, in Dachau.

Genia knew no one was left. At first, she had asked everyone she met, "Where were you?" She described her mother's coat with the seal collar, her father's mustache, Jesse's straight brown hair and the blue mittens she had knit for him. She found one young woman from Czestochowa who had been on the same line.

"Auschwitz," she whispered. That was all. She told Genia that her own life had been saved by a German soldier who delivered her to a Polish farmer to clean stables.

Uncle Lolek brought Genia to his cramped apartment in Czestochowa, where he nursed her back to health. For weeks while the pneumonia raged in her lungs, racking her whole body with heaving coughs, she thought of strawberries. She had imagined them as she stood staring at the assembly line of gun shells in the labor camp. To taste *truskawki!* Fresh strawberries!

Oh, she longed to be clean and pretty with new teeth. Uncle Lolek had promised when she felt better, her teeth would be fixed. In the *lager,* they had rotted and turned black. Her hair had been thick, shiny like taffeta. She pulled at the razed strands that they might grow out quickly so she could roll her hair like the American actresses.

When Genia was well enough to travel, she went back to her family's house, Number Seven Mokotowska in Warsaw. Hadn't Premier Mikowlajczyk announced on the radio: "Every Polish citizen who returns to Poland will be welcomed"?

Just as her father had instructed them all before they left, she removed the wooden floorboard behind the boiler in the basement. She heard something. The care-taker, Andresz, who had known the family before the war, had followed her downstairs.

He stood there, his gold tooth glinting in the shadow of the thick overhead pipes. "You found something," he said.

She held several diamond rings, her father's cigarette case. She moved away from him, trying to hide behind the coal-burning boiler, which excreted smoke in obscene rumbles.

"I thought they gassed all of you," he said, stepping toward her.

"Don't!" she cried, terrified, backing into the wall.

His steps echoed. "You don't live here anymore. I'll tell the *polizia* that you are stealing—"

She handed him her mother's engagement ring with the tear-shaped diamond, then tried to hide the rest behind her back.

He pocketed it. Then moved closer.

"Please—"

"One more or I'll call—"

She gave him a smaller diamond. And ran.

In a small striped suitcase, she carried her family's wealth. She took a *drozka* to the big boulevard Marszalkowska with the fancy stores. Warsaw hadn't changed. People still promenaded in all their finery, but she recognized no one. Couples drank tea with strawberry jam from steaming glasses in Cafe Ziemianska where Tata would take her for cherry tarts. Their laughter stabbed as she looked down at her own clothes. At least now she didn't wear the yellow star.

Having sold the diamonds, Genia had new brassieres and underwear sewn, dresses with pearl buttons, leather shoes. The color had returned to her skin, her legs were shaven, and she menstruated again. She had not bled during her years in the *lager*.

She found Janek's address from the Warsaw Jewish Agency. When he opened the door, Genia smiled. "Do you see anything?"

He admired her new teeth, she, his glass eye.

They went to a fine restaurant on Marszalkowska where they ate corned beef with horseradish and *kapusta,* cabbage. As he drank Russian vodka, arranging the shot glasses like a pyramid, she sipped blackberry brandy, protesting that it went to her feet. Then they returned to his small room, several blocks from where her family's apartment had been, and made love.

Genia bought him a suit of navy wool with thin gray stripes like Tata used to sell. He looked like a gentleman. They went to concerts of Liszt and Chopin, and finally, because he was her tattooed lover, she had no other, she bought him a motorcycle. When they waltzed, he dipped her body, his hand secure against the small of her back. As her head fell back, her hair flying behind her, she thought of herself as Rita Hayworth in *Gilda*.

After a few months, the money vanished. *Pouf!* So did Janek and his German girlfriend, Fraulein Helga, with her blond hair and common features, on the motorcycle.

All that remained was her father's cigarette case. Genia returned to Czestochowa to live with her uncle Lolek and his new wife, Fela, his dead wife's younger sister.

Lying down on the small pallet in what had once been the maid's room, Genia closed her eyes. Ever she is startled by the beauty of his features, her lover, whose demeanor is manly, the glossy black hairs under his arms, his thick beard. He is powerful, a partisan fighter, a hero. The one who will carry her from Uncle Lolek's house, marry her.

"We'll be together forever," she whispers. "You'll be my Momma. Tata. And my Jesse."

SURVIVORS DANCE

The Czestochowa Society of Heroes, Martyrs, and Refugees had decorated the community room with pink crepe paper and silver foil stars. Genia heard the American song "Funny Face" as she entered the room. Several couples were dancing.

That's when she spotted him. The beautiful, dark-haired man, standing alone. He wore a navy blue suit several sizes too large, his jacket suspended as from a wire hanger. His cuffs covered his scuffed shoes. But he was handsome. Like Tyrone Power. She shifted her weight from foot to foot. Summoning the courage of her new teeth, she smiled so they glistened in all their porcelain patina, just as her eyes did.

Heniek turned away. It was too late. Too late for him to be standing there like a debutante at a ball, but his boss's partner Marek had insisted. Inside his pockets, his fingers snapped like firecrackers.

Women were seeing him again. Before when he weighed hardly forty-seven kilos, he was invisible. Now, having eaten a full loaf of *chleb,* dark bread, every day since the liberation, he had gained twenty-five kilos in four months. But he had to be careful. Shimon's friend, Holzmann, had eaten flanken, potato *galuskas*, carrots and plums, drinking *piwo* by the pitcher. He wouldn't stop even when they tried to take his plate away. "*Glodny!*" he screamed. "Hunger!" His intestines exploded.

Genia went to the bathroom. When she returned, he stood in the same place. She sashayed past him so he could smell her perfume, Evening in Paris. Slowly she moved, wanting to meet his eyes, but shy. Maybe he was married. Maybe he wasn't normal from the war. Her feet hurt in her new black leather pumps.

Didn't this girl know that he, like most of the men, had forgotten or rather, this no longer interested him? For months and years, they had played dead. They were called *Musselman*, not men, sheep, their skin a fish-gray pallor.

I must wait until I am chosen. Genia fingered the white lace on her collar. As I was chosen by the Polish policeman who searched the Selection line, "Where's the girl with the white kerchief?" *Does he see me?* Now he was looking at her. She smiled shyly.

This lovely girl with brown waves and shiny green eyes wanted him. Heniek hadn't had a woman in such a long time. Except Tonia, immediately after liberation. The mole on the inside of her thigh had identified her in a heap of dead bodies.

This one in the navy dress with a white lace collar was a schoolgirl. Did she know? Of existing on nerves, obedient but watchful for the moment when he could escape, leaving behind his brother, Yacob, to die in the dark, sealed basement of potatoes, where only those who clawed to the crack under the door could breathe.

His eyes traveled to one place. Not her breasts or legs, between her legs, the roundness of her ass. He stared at the white skin inside her arm. This was a reflex, as an unmarried woman might look down to see if the man who has approached is wearing a wedding band. He moved a step to scrutinize her other arm. White as the damask on his mother's Sabbath table.

They were different, the ones with numbers. The numbers meant they would live if they could work. B48356. He felt for the blue tattoo branding the tender inside of his arm. Daily, the numbered ones stepped over the dead, picked through, defiled them for their own survival. Heniek felt the charred tips of his fingers hidden inside his pockets.

Anyway, she had been somewhere too. Jewish girls who spent the war at school, as young wives and mothers, who became nurses, *rebbitzen* were not members of the Czestochowa survivors social club.

He studied this motherless, fatherless waif who had survived by a hangnail, like all of them, and wondered at her smile, which was open and hopeful. Finally he approached.

They danced to "Love Me or Leave Me" sung by Doris Day. He was stiff. She suggested they *spatzier*, stroll.

Outside, he seemed easier, but so silent. She chattered about her English lessons and how she hoped to study medicine in the United States. He said that he worked for his cousin, vague about the exact nature of his job. Something to do with money.

They stood on a dark corner. A prosperous Polish couple walked past them with a white sheared poodle on a leash. "*Zyd*," the woman whispered to her husband. *Jew.*

"What are *they* doing here?" the man demanded indignantly.

Heniek and Genia were silent for several moments after the Polish couple had disappeared around the corner. "You heard?" Heniek dropped his voice. "More killed in Radom last week?"

"They didn't destroy enough of us? *Cholera yasne!*" she cursed bitterly.

He took her in his arms. She allowed him to hold her as she told him about the white kerchief.

"Where did they send you?" Heniek asked.

"Hasag Hugo Schneider. I worked in the assembly line, cleaning gun shells. And you?"

"Lodz ghetto. Until the *Aktion*," he answered bluntly. "Then Auschwitz."

She took a breath. "Auschwitz," she repeated the word. "It's a miracle."

"Have you ever watched a cockroach? How they know your finger is behind them. How they burrow their bodies into any crevices in the wall, under the floorboard, make that squeaking sound. That's what I was like. I knew how to survive. That's all."

Slowly, they walked together, past Alleya 1. "This is where my family hid during the war," she said. "Until they came to our apartment, rounded us up." She showed him the market square where they had lined up for Selection. "We were the last building on the street, so I had watched for days."

"The beauty contest," he said.

She nodded. "I stay with my uncle Lolek now."

They stood outside her uncle's building with the torn awning. "I'll come back to Czestochowa to see you next week," he promised.

Genia watched Heniek's back as he walked away. Would he return? She thought of Janek, her *lager* "husband," who had abandoned her for a *Niemka*, a German woman, after spending most of her money.

Heniek came back the next week, and the weeks after. They desired each other as often as they could steal moments, Uncle Lolek at work, Fela shopping, throwing off their clothes, throwing themselves against each other, bones clanging with hunger.

As soon as they finished, it began again, for as long as he could, and there was never enough. She wanted to lose herself, melt into him, his arms forcing hers above her head. They married four months later.

On a Saturday night in December 1945, Uncle Lolek gave her away. Genia wore Srola Federman's navy blue dress, her hair rolled in a crown of white orchids. "The voice of mirth and the voice of gladness, the voice of the bridegroom and the voice of the bride." They stood under a chuppah, made of wooden two by fours and wrapped in a white *tallit*.

Heniek crushed a wine glass with the heel of his shoe and sang in Hebrew and Polish, and all the men joined in *"Di Yiddishe Partizanerin"* as they carried him in a chair. The Czestochowa Society of Heroes, Martyrs, and Refugees contributed a whole beef shank.

Fela grabbed her hand suddenly. "Genushka, you don't have a mommy to tell you things you should know. So listen to me," she whispered in her ear. "I'm a little bit older, so maybe I know something."

Genia tried to move away from her overpowering scent of dried rose petals. Fela's hold grew tighter. "Don't get him used to it too much or he won't leave you alone." She patted Genia's hand.

They took the train, second-class, to Tsopot on the Baltic Sea. They rarely left their hotel room. As she watched Heniek shave, Genia envied his razor, wishing it were her tongue, wishing they could stay in this room forever.

After a few days, they came to Lodz, where Heniek once lived with his parents. A Polish family occupied his apartment. There was nowhere to go. Besides, there were pogroms. Jews murdered on the streets.

Heniek paid someone who knew someone fifty dollars. Genia crawled on her stomach behind Heniek, hiding under a stack of mattresses on a flatbed truck. Several hours later, they crossed the border to safety—into Germany.

OUR FATHER, OUR KING

My number is 174517; we have been baptized; we will carry the tattoo on our left arm until we die. —Primo Levi

My father stands in front of the meter where his maroon Chevy is parked. His American clothes hang on a wiry frame, plaid jacket, artless brown trousers.

He checks his watch again with a jagged flick of his wrist. Is he waiting for someone? An illicit, uncatered affair? Heniek Palovsky *shtupping* Stella Markovitz? Ha! My father never looks at women, young, old, chesty, a succulent Jewish piece of ass. Only at my mother, whom he bosses and belittles: "Genia, you're stupid. Do you understand? Your mother doesn't know nothing," he tells me.

Her handsome prince, who smothers his black curls in her torn stocking. He wraps it around his head to straighten his hair, which makes him look like a shrunken head.

All Genia's ideas of working out of the house are crushed like cigarette butts. "I'll pay more taxes than you can earn." She turns her immense energies terrifyingly toward me and burns my father's dinners. But he struts with rooster pride when she drapes the mink stole he bought around her white shoulders. When she leaves for several days to visit the thinnest branches of her dead family tree, he goes hungry, unshaven, pines for her like a stray.

What is he doing? What am I doing? I've come home to visit. I stand rapt at the corner of 161st Street and Fort Washington Avenue, as I did when I was a child, watching my unknowable father.

He worked long hours as a factory foreman. Sometimes, late at night, I saw a phantom stalk heavy-footed past my room to the toilet.

Daddy! "Why aren't you sleeping?" Daddy! "Genia, make her go to sleep!"

I hid from him in the hallway closet that was deep and dark, a forest of coats, shoes and boots below. "I know you're in there. Open the door! Zosha! Before you make me mad." I slowly opened the door. A crack. Dad? I held my breath. Suddenly, he leapt up, waving his arms wildly, shouting, "Ah ha!"

As I stand here, time burns. Burns. Burning. The two quarters between his fingers like wheels going nowhere, the hot metal as if he could make fire. He glances at the silver parking meter with its crucifying arrow, edging to the red zone. In eight minutes, time will run out. Then Heniek will be free. He drops the quarters back into his jacket pocket. Genia fixed it, but the weight of change rips the lining again.

Last week, he got to the parking meter five minutes late. He checked his watch. But the cop got there first, waiting for the moment when the quarter ran out in the parking meter. A woman with black shoes. She shook her head as she wrote the ticket. "License number?" she demanded. "This is my license," he answered. He undid his sleeve, showing her his mark: B48356.

"I don't care if you got a tattoo."

Bitch. Sometimes they were the worst. Kicking where it hurt, their laughter the hiss of ice. They weren't actually women. They didn't have what all women have—hearts. His sisters, Rutka and Perele, who was pregnant. He looks around himself. Where are the fancy people with their doormen and dogs that get better than him? All the world is a hotel for transients in Harlem.

He peers down the street. You have to have the cunning of the camps around here. A black junkie hawks his kid's schoolbooks. The man who paints the missing hairs on his scalp with bootblack, playing a set of invisible drums with wooden sticks. "Gene Krupa lives!" he shouts. A madhouse. Cops marching around like Gestapo with their nightsticks, pistols in black leather belts. And they're great writers. Like Jack London! Writing tickets of twenty-five, fifty, even one hundred dollars while people are murdering each other down the street. They can even take your car away.

Then how would he work? How could he earn enough money to feed his family? It tires him to think of it. So tired. *I am a man who has seen suffering.* He does not sleep at night except a few minutes before he must awake. Luckily, the ticket was for only twenty-five dollars, which he'll pay. He can afford it. Six minutes only.

What's six minutes? Where has he to rush? The grave. So he is tight. He knows. The Talmud says: A miser is like a mouse, which lies on coins. But if he has a dollar in his pocket and spends it, not for luxuries, but for what they need, he has tears in his eyes because he knows he has less. I'm too old to change. Five minutes, almost.

Money. That's the only real thing there is in this life. All the rest is for philosophers and rabbis. His foot taps the base of the parking meter. Let them count how many mangled angels' limbs can fit on a pinhead. Any fool could shoot a bullet through the most brilliant brain. He was a nothing and yet he lived. Was it God who chose him to make a fool of them all? *Tap, tap.*

The one they called Pushkin because he recited love poems, writing with match carbon on his arm. Murdered. With money you could buy time, a *shtickel* bread, soup like from a sewer. *Tap, tap.* He would have killed for it. Not to die. And now he lets the moments burn like kindling. Fool! *Thou scarest me with dreams, and terrify me through visions: so that my soul chooseth strangling, and death rather than these my bones.* Time is money. If only he had as much money as he has time.

He grasps his stomach, chronically constipated so that each movement of his bowels is an ordeal. Genia humiliates him, gives him no privacy, bursting in on him as he tries, so painful, pressing his hands on the sides of the seat, pushing, squeezing his sphincter, which aches to empty. Nothing. It stays inside him like all the hatred he felt, growing harder, the insidious turd. *Tap, tap, tap.*

Why died I not in the womb? Why did I not give up the ghost when I came out of the belly? Why did the knee receive me? Why the breasts that I should suck? Job's curses boom in his ears as he waits for the time to run out in the goddamn parking meter. *Why is the light given to a man whose way is hid, and whom God hath hedged in?*

They have bread on the table. That's what matters. Bread, not death. I will not die. He had said it so many times, he believed it. Though everyone else died. He had craved bread the way others hallucinated messiahs. Black pumpernickel, rye, sourdough, oh, challah, sweetest of breads.

How his father salted the Sabbath challah with a silver minaret shaker, breaking off a piece that he shared with them all. His brother Yacob's paunch was like a pickle barrel. Heniek smiled. Praying in his white *tallit* with the navy threads, a black satin *yarmulke* covering his bent head. Yacob's rhythm was sluggish, a devout but lazy swishing like water in a beaker, reciting the prayer by rote. Heniek had stood next to him, long-legged, sharp-featured, severe in the bones of his shoulders, holding his back like a steel door.

Flicking his wrist, Heniek peers at his watch, eyes trekking the second hand's orbit. Four minutes. Why didn't he finish with it already? *Tap, tap.* Drop the quarters in the slot. He shakes his head, unwilling to give in.

Once, he had been a *cheder bucher*, destined, perhaps, to follow his famous *zeyde*, Rebbe Avraham Rubinsky of Redomansk. He had imagined his days spent as he had seen his grandfather with his cabalistic computations, numerology of the faith-keepers: to sanctify all that existed, even the serpent. His grandfather's impeccable finger, smooth as a baby's, moving slowly down the page as if it were Braille, as if he could feel the black seraphim of the Hebrew characters.

/   /   /

I cry to you, Blessed One, my Rock. Do not be deaf to me.
For if you are silent, I shall go down to the pit like the rest.

Grandfather Rebbe Avraham Rubinsky recited David's psalms from memory. *"Have mercy upon me for I am withered away. O Lord, heal me for my bones are vexed."* He was called Avraham Tehillim Zager. His *zeyde*, the psalmsayer, had opened his heart, all his senses and God's tongue filled him with an ecstasy Heniek would never know. When his grandfather was too weak to pray, he held onto the *bima* with the Torah scroll, the black Hebraic characters oversized for the cantor of the synagogue. But he couldn't see. His eyes slivers of blue, new moons floating in a milky sea.

The thin vessel of his grandfather, his fingers glass thimbles, shivered as they sent him to the right, the line with the other grandmothers and grandfathers. They would be taken to sanitariums in the green mountains where the fresh air would restore them.

How instinct raw as a fang had flung Heniek from the death march into a dank gully in the woods. He had watched them continue, Yacob, still innocent of his brother's abandonment. He couldn't call to him. Three minutes more. I am banished from my home, God, famished.

In Auschwitz, there wasn't to eat or sleep. Sanity was a piece of soap. They wanted to fill us with horror toward our own flesh. How he did hand-to-hand battle with despair, which would have reduced him to *Musselman*, the breathing dead whose backs were rounded like beasts of unbearable burden. The first ones to go. They wanted to get rid of all the useless eaters. Beautify the human race.

In Auschwitz, he lit four matches instead of *yortzeit* candles and recited Kaddish for his parents, his two beautiful sisters, Rutka, the proud one with the long braid wound around her head, and the younger, small-boned and delicate Perele. Yacob was still alive, he heard, though in a different part of the camp. The matches had burned. He let them brand his *neshuma*. His soul.

B48356. A good number. It meant they wanted us to live so we could work. The ones without numbers went straight to the gas. Why should they bother with them? Luckily, I was in the kitchen. I could trade scraps. *Arbeit Macht Frei.*

Heniek, I am called. Henry in English. You took me to the wilderness to slay me. The knife glinted like a rabid dog's teeth as you raised your hand. Why did you stop as I lay bound on your altar of wood, barbed wire around me? *Lay not thine hand upon the lad, neither do thou anything unto him: for now I know that thou fearest God, seeing thou hast not withheld thy son, thine only son from me.*

Avinu Malkenu. You don't exist. *Our Father, Our King.* You never existed. There is no You even to discuss. A psycho screeches "Gene Krupa lives!" You. You. What's You? Nothing. A void filled with lies. Liar! It makes him crazy.

On Riverside Drive, a man in a brown toupee like an animal on his head approached. "You are Heniek, no? Had you a brother, Yacob?" He nodded. "In Auschwitz?" So? "I thought it was you. It's okay, you don't recognize Yonkileh. I was younger then, with a physique." He laughed at his own belly after near-starvation and dysentery. *Nu,* Heniek had mumbled without affect. "You remember how it was snow on the ground? None of us had what to wear so we wrapped newspaper on our feet. They marched us to a farmhouse with chickens making so much noise. The cellar where the farmer kept his potatoes, there was no air, so the potatoes wouldn't rot. That's where they put us to die. Except me, and I don't know if you remember, Marek. We forced our mouths to the crack under the door. That's how we breathed. Yacob, I'm sorry to say it, he was in the back."

No! He should let Yacob rest in the silence of his bones. No grave. None of them. Left to die like trash after a picnic, everything empty, layers of skin flapping like plastic bags. Finished.

Heniek turns to watch the *kapo* across the street. She is writing in her black notebook. She could destroy him if she wanted to. He checks the parking meter. It is over. But he remains standing as if frozen another minute, will not give *them* the satisfaction. Then he drops two quarters into the slot. When the light turns green, Heniek looks in both directions, then crosses the street to return home. Though I left years ago, I follow behind him.

THE BIG H

"I hesitate to speak tonight about the subject of the Symposium. It is one of such horror that despite the fact that it happened so many years ago, I believe we still turn away from it in horror; except for those brave poets, writers, artists, and musicians who have dared to look into its depths and depict the reality of Auschwitz . . . "

The Right Reverend Paul Moore, Jr., Episcopal Bishop of New York, gave the keynote address to the first interfaith Holocaust conference. *Auschwitz: Beginning of a New Era.* It was 1974.

"I believe that we tread on holy ground tonight. This too I hesitate to touch. I take off my shoes lest by walking on it I somehow destroy the fragility, the holiness, of that ground. I am referring to our sharing, as fellow human beings, the strange glory of innocent suffering, the strange glory of heroism, which came out of the stories of Auschwitz.

"This innocent suffering is a strange thing in our creation, and Auschwitz may well be its greatest symbol. Perhaps there is some mystery of atonement here. Perhaps this cosmic power of the Holy Innocents can be a means by which we become one. And so I bow down and worship before that innocent suffering and innocent death."

For hours, I had been sitting in a hard wooden pew at St. John the Divine, recrossing my legs on the padded kneeling platform, surrounded by carved figures of devotion. I glared at the black Book of Common Prayer with its golden cross, thinking of how my mother recoiled at the sight of crucifixes. "Let *him* burn on *his* cross," she spewed as she scrubbed her oven, waxed her linoleum.

Poles got drunk on Christmas and Easter, my mother told me. Once as she was returning from a sleepover at her cousin Clara's, two soldiers chased after her, calling, "*Zyd!*" Jew! Whore! She ran as fast as her skinny legs would take her. *Please!* She kept running until they caught her.

"You Jews live like pigs. Look how filthy the street is. Clean it," the smaller man commanded.

"I have nothing to clean with," she whispered.

"Use your dress," the one with the pistol said.

"Heavy shit, huh?" I whispered, nudging Christine, who sat next to me, listening intently.

Born Catholic, married to a Jew, Christine couldn't get enough of us, our food, our writers, our Yiddish expressions. She called herself a Judeophile, a Jew hag. "I had never met a single Jew in Winnipeg," she once told me. "*You* were such a revelation to me!" Despite my repeated instruction, Christine pronounced *kvetch* as if it had two syllables. She met my eyes momentarily, then shifted her attention reverently.

Sure, I too was awed, felt outclassed, outcast, having imagined the Holocaust mostly my own bogeyman and a handful of survivors, my parents and their foreign-accented cronies from the DP camps. There was a write-up on yesterday's editorial page of the *New York Times*.

There is, in fact, no way to abolish from the mind the demons of what this symposium called "the Nazi machinery of death." The numbers branded on the arms of death camps survivors have not faded with the years. Neither must the shame of those who so branded their fellow men, women, and children be allowed to fade from memory, lest the forces of darkness once again find humanity off-guard against man's capacity for evil.

Yes, it was sublime. I gazed around the Cathedral of St. John the Divine. Laser-thin beams bisected tall stone columns in the darkness, illuminating slivers of exquisitely tinted glass. Tapestries of Calvary. The pulpit surrounded by filigree of latticework, glowing in the light like summer raindrops. First-class, five-star real estate.

I thought of the drafty *shtibel* on the second floor of a tenement on 158th Street, where my father prayed. A torn fiberglass curtain separated the men from the women, who peered hungrily through the holes. I could see my father, his cheeks glowing as he *dovened*, swaying back and forth, his lips moving silently.

As I sat in this crypt with its nativity statues, so tender, all I could feel was a cold hatred of all the insidious privilege here. Everything so tall and silent. I hated them for their generations of family, of a lived history, for "My great-grandparents came over on the *Mayflower*." My parents came over with hundreds of dirty, despised DPs on the *General Hersey*. A distant organ's note reverberated in the nave.

He could have been the president of a university in his dark, bell-sleeved robe. This could be graduation. From the white alabaster pulpit, Bishop Paul Moore's voice rose, swelling to fill the cathedral.

"So let it be. Let it be. Let us listen with our hearts and with our souls to the cries of anguish. Let those cries and let that vision not be wasted, and let us take it up once more so that the very things which for so long have been barriers between Christian and Jew, between brother and sister, may now become a means that binds us together."

He paused dramatically, modulating to a stage whisper. "For the time is short, very short." Then his voice rose again, "I am grateful to all those who will lift up for us something of this vision."

Bowing his head, the light glinted in tiny arrows off the strands of his fierce silver hair. Was this *deus ex machina* or what?

Dean James Morton greeted the bishop as he climbed down from the pulpit. Of the younger, hipper clergy school, he wore a crewneck sweater over his collar, his wry smile a tad worldly.

As Dean Morton began his introductions, Christine leaned over and whispered, "When did he say you could read?"

"After everyone else."

Earlier that day, I had approached him. Dean Morton was not happy about my request to read my poems, but reluctantly agreed I could follow the scheduled speakers.

Now I held my sheaf of poems on my lap, fingers tapping the black cardboard binder, tapping two-three-four like a piano exercise.

"Aren't you terrified?" she asked.

"It's more terrifying not to read them." I looked at her, smiled to dilute my nerves. Tap, tap.

I was a medium, Houdini of the Holocaust, which transmitted itself through me, the uncut umbilical cord of my mother feeding me blood images vivid as they were terrifying. Spirits of the dead cried out of me.

My parents sought the anonymous quiet of Washington Heights, except in the close quarters of others like themselves, there being safety in silence and invisibility. But I strove for recognition. It was like the gift of light and life.

Besides, the Holocaust was mine—except for the survivors. It was an exclusive club. No Johnny-come-lately academic, theologian, or artist should be allowed to cash in on my private cache of suffering and obsession.

I was born on the other side, lived my first year in a German Displaced Persons camp. I would show them what it meant to have one's kin extinguished in history's bonfire, and the only living family singed at their source so all that released itself with the exuberance of nature came slow and with great difficulty.

I would show the ones in cozy chairs in Holocaust Studies like Uly Oppenheim at the Postgraduate Center, radical prof/prophet with long gray hair and well-fitting jeans. He had read the day before from his seminal study in survival, *Our Bodies, Not Our Souls*, a collection of interviews with women who shamefully admitted their enforced prostitution in Nazi brothels. Now he sat across the aisle, slumped in his seat, occasionally jotting on a small leather-bound pad.

I noted the gaggle of Guggenheim and Fulbright fellows, Library of Congress poets, recipients of National Endowment for the Arts grants who in search of the loaded metaphor like a Saturday night special—pull the trigger and scorch—dredged up a fandango of barbed wire, black boots, and Nazi lampshades. What did they know besides their bleeding footnotes?

The Holocaust was mine alone to bear. That's why they had to hear me. I'd show all these merchants what it meant to suffer, or to be so close to it that you got a dose.

I turned to Christine. Her eyes were filled with tears as she listened to a dark-haired man in a *yarmulke* speak about Israel's legacy. "Our land was created from the ashes and we must never forget that," he declared. "Not for a moment. And we must teach our children and their children . . . "

Next, a dour, middle-aged former nun stood in front of the gallery. "We must look at the very roots of Christian theology," she began stiffly. "And there shall we discover the roots of Jewish hatred."

God, I had never heard so much talk of suffering, sacrificial lambs, martyrs, and unspeakable horrors mounted in such a scholarly drone.

Dead time. Time of the dead. The silence thick with howling. Dead time. Bed time. I don't want to go to sleep.

I heard applause, looked up to see a famous American poet from Boston mount the pulpit, his silver hair winged victoriously on either side of his head. He read from his latest book, *Auschwitz Sonnets,* inspired by his visit to the concentration camp.

"He's the last speaker." Christina pointed to the program. "You'll be next."

"Oh." I looked around the cathedral, the large, silent audience.

"Nervous?" she asked.

I shook my head, but my stomach revolted. Two-three-four! Two-three-four! Cold fingers rapping the binder. Tapping.

Polite applause.

He joined the other speakers in the front pew. Dean Morton had stepped down. He was shaking hands, thanking people. He hadn't said anything yet. I peered around myself. He said he would. He had to. I waited. Patiently. I was waiting for Dean Morton to announce my reading.

People started getting up, putting on their coats. Then Dean Morton walked up the aisle, past me, unseeing. The speakers followed behind him.

"He said he would introduce me!" I cried. More and more people were leaving. "What should I do?"

I couldn't believe it. Once again, a Jew abandoned by the Church. *He had said I could read!*

With all my ambition and grit, grinding my teeth so my jaw ached with longing, I wanted to do it. Tell their story, which was mine too. Remember. Yes. Get it out like some web-fingered demon child.

Our parents survived to bear witness. We, in turn, must be their attestors. Testify!

"What can you do?" Christine shrugged.

If I was truly the Holocaust Kid, living for it, saving myself like a virgin bride for the occasion of my deflowering, now was the time. I was in love with the war, memorized every detail, milking it for all its horror. I wanted to be there. My father's Auschwitz, my mother's Czestochowa. To burn in the purifying fires.

"Them's the breaks, kid," Christine added sympathetically.

"No!" I cried, rising, climbing over her legs.

Someone would hear me, dammit. This was my moment. I would stand at the pulpit of this church and recite my poetry. I ran up on the stage, clutching my black cardboard binder.

"Just a moment," I grabbed the microphone with a white-knuckled grasp, my binder of poems in the other hand. "Please! I have some poems I've written—" I began.

People stopped in the center aisle. All eyes on the madwoman. The spotlight fixed me in its yellow star.

"I am the first-born daughter of Heniek and Genia Palovsky," I said, voice twig-thin. "Both Holocaust survivors. My father was in Auschwitz. 'A Tattooed Dreamer—'" I began to read slowly, halting at the end of each line.

> *We dream we are there.*
> *We hear the Gestapo shout, "Raus!"*
> *We stand on line*
>
> *Waiting to be selected*
> *Left side or right.*
>
> *We dream we suffer*
> *Real things.*

I paused. The audience shifted impatiently. Those near the door headed out. The scholars never returned. A few others, curious, waited to see what would happen. I could see Dean Morton pacing in the back nervously.

> *Would you sell my hand*
> *as an ashtray*

tapered fingers
perfectly formed
for cigarettes.

Would you sell my ears
as paperweights
matching conches
expertly carved
to contain clips.

More people walked out. It was an exodus! The doors slammed noisily. I would not stop. Words had power. I declaimed over the din.

Would you sell my skin
hair shaven
softer than chamois
to reupholster
chairs.

Well, I had managed to empty the house. But I didn't care. Raising my voice, I went right on. "This is the first poem I ever wrote. 'Child of the Holocaust.'"

Six million Jews died
the figure was commanded
to where normal children keep
1492, 1776, the Alamo.

I wanted to forget
every digit of the six million
the numerals etched into your arm
like a phone number.

As I sucked your milk, I counted
gassed men, women, infants—
Zyklon B came up again
and again as phlegm.

Six million Jews died
and I was born
a child of the universe
always, a child of the Holocaust.

Afterward, there was silence. Dank, acidic silence, as if I had performed an obscene act in public. Maybe I had. Stripping in the presence of the Holiest of Holies, the Big H. They despised me. My heart revved. Shame. My ego, which had ballooned to fill the stage, deflated to a mite. What was I trying to prove?

I thought of my mother's words: "Don't stick out like a sore thumb. Just be normal! Not worse, but average. It's better that people don't know too much. Nobody likes a show-off. Stand out of the line and someone shoots you. Just be normal."

That's when Christine rushed up and embraced me. "You did it!" she cried. "God, you really do have balls!"

All I could feel was my own skinless vulnerability. "But everyone walked out."

"Some people stayed."

I still didn't stir. Christine shook me. "Zosha, you were very good."

I wanted to sob as I held onto her, squeezing my eyes shut. A miserable choke-back-tears shame. I took a deep breath. "Thanks," I whispered in her ear.

When I opened my eyes, I could see a young woman striding determinedly down the aisle to speak to me.

"I understand," she said, touching my arm softly. "I am a child of the Holocaust too."

Her eyes burned with a crazy intensity I recognized. "My mother went through the camps . . . " she told me.

I nodded.

"Do you go to any Second Generation groups?" she asked.

"No," I answered.

"Maryse Ehrlich," she introduced herself.

Her hair was long and dark like mine, but she wore too much makeup. Lips painted bright red, her eyelids smudged kohl. It made her look clownish. Was this my *doppelgänger,* I wondered. The double we fear in a funhouse mirror, never funny though. *My sister.*

I looked at Christine, then back at the woman. Her dark brown eyes blazed as she spoke, but her tone was flat. "My mother was in Belsen with her sister, who didn't survive the war. My mother did, but she never got over it."

"I understand," I said to shut her up. This came with the territory too. Listening to other people's Holocaust stories.

"Do you?" She paused. "Wherever she was, she always worried. She was convinced she left the gas jets on in the stove."

I shifted uncomfortably.

"My mother died three years ago," she went on, her voice matter-of-fact. "It might as well have been a suicide. There were photographs of the camps taped to the wall next to her bed. She had constructed shrines. Little stacks of eyeglasses, teeth—"

"Enough, please," I said finally. "I have to go."

"Of course," she said, slowly moving away. "I won't keep you. But I wanted to give you something."

She passed me a folded sheet of paper. A flyer for her reading with the date and name of a performance space downtown. "I'll leave two tickets for you at the door," she said. "How do you spell your name?"

She scared the hell out of me, but I told her.

"Good. I'll see you soon," she said, jotting my name down on a small pad. Then she took my hand in hers. "We have much to share." She looked intently into my eyes. "I feel we could be friends."

I tried to disengage myself, but her grip was strong.

Afterward, I watched as she strode up the center aisle of the church. She wore black tights with a hole at the heel. Her dancer's wraparound skirt slowly unraveled, the hem trailing behind her in a train. Though she held her body erect, it was fleshy, letting out the secrets of our coven.

"No, we don't," I said when she was out of earshot. "We don't share anything. What is it about New York City?" I demanded. "You do something and your only audience gives you a paper about what *she's* doing."

"Even if you're one in a million, there's still nine of you in the city," Christine reminded me. "Can I see her flyer?"

I took the sheet from my pocket, reading aloud: "*Exorcisms: Rituals of Remembrance and Revenge.*" I rolled my eyes.

"What?" Christine asked.

"Why the hell did I put myself out there?" I demanded. "I could've just sat quietly in my seat."

"You?" Christine laughed. "I don't think so."

As we walked up the center aisle of the cathedral, devotional shards of colored glass flashed in the rose window. I crumpled Maryse's flyer into a smaller and smaller ball, then stuck it into my pocketbook. Looking down, I noticed a gold disk with a crucifix on the marble floor. Raised gold letters encircled the gold cross: WHOSOEVER DRINKETH OF THE WATER THAT I SHALL GIVE THEM SHALL NEVER THIRST.

SHOAH CASANOVA

Uly Oppenheim, Ph.D., actually looked like the photograph on the back of *Our Bodies, Not Our Souls.* He was a darkly arrogant man with Byronic hair, beak nose. Tough wrestler's stance at the podium like a young Norman Mailer. This was Jewish macho: aggressive, assaulting intelligence.

As he stepped down from the stage of the Postgraduate Center, he was met by a crush of admirers, colleagues, and Shoah professionals.

"Of course, I'm saying Jews are *meshuggeh*," he declared. "Consider our collective trauma over the millennia, ending in the ultimate paranoid fantasy . . . "

I had strutted my smart stuff toward the stage, hoping the professor might notice a young woman in a short leather skirt, clingy red sweater. The effect was intellectual, I imagined. Ayn Rand, née Alice Rosenbaum. A Jewess greenhorn like me, born in Russia.

Not that I wanted to sleep with Uly Oppenheim. I wasn't a groupie. But without my piquing his sexual interest, he would never talk to me. I was twenty-seven years old and how else was I ever going to learn *anything*? Professor Oppenheim could teach me volumes.

An older woman with dyed red hair and dangling Mexican turquoise earrings whispered something in his ear that made him laugh. For several minutes, they exchanged gossip about The Holocaust as Metaphor seminar in Frankfurt.

I walked over to a nearby table and picked up his book. The cover, lipstick red, displayed a black garter with a swastika. Leafing through the pages of *Our Bodies, Not Our Souls,* I discovered that each chapter began with a different name. "Gertrud F." "Eva Z." "Alicia W." All were women. All had spent time in Nazi brothels.

"Would you like me to sign it?" he asked.

"You must be kidding!" I faced him. "This is pornography. Interviewing women Holocaust survivors—" I put the book down angrily.

"The war was pornography," he answered. "I'm just a historian."

"But why tell this story?" I insisted. "It's awful."

"Are you a therapist?" he asked.

"Me?" I gasped. "Do I look like one?"

At that moment, he appraised me. Like a chicken in plastic wrap. Shaking his head, he said, "No. It's just that's who comes to my lectures. And the survivors, of course. Why'd you come?"

"I'm a writer," I declared. "Like you."

"What are you working on?"

"I don't like to talk about it. I don't mean to sound mysterious," I said. "It's just that every time you open the oven, it gets—"

"Let's go outside," he said, taking my arm firmly. "I just have to find my briefcase."

I felt the prick of eyes upon us. The red-haired woman whispered something to a brunette in a tight French braid. Both were dressed in black like Greek widows. Their eyes followed us as we walked out together.

He could have had any woman in that room, but he had selected me. It was a warm March evening.

"Let me understand this," he said. "You make up stories about movie stars?" We walked up Sixth Avenue.

"That's what fan magazines are about," I explained. "You take the biggest stars. Actually they're not all stars. Like Jackie and Ari Onassis. But Liz Taylor always sells. And Elvis."

He appeared confused.

"My latest masterpiece is 'Elvis's Secret Words from the Grave.' In the June issue of *Movie Screen*.'"

"How do you write these?" he asked.

"I read Earl Wilson, Liz Smith, Marilyn Beck," I answered matter-of-factly. "Like right now I have to write a piece: 'Cher's Secret Hours in the Dark with Robert Redford.'"

"But isn't she still with Sonny?"

"You see." I grinned. "Everyone's contemptuous, but even you know about the stars. Anyway, I'll describe Cher's deep inner thoughts and feelings as she watched Redford's newest film."

"Do you have fantasies about the stars?"

I looked at him. "Of course not. But I have to pay my bills." "I guess you could call me a literary slut." I shrugged.

"Where'd you get that mouth?"

I didn't answer him. We continued to walk uptown until we stood in front of my brownstone building on West Seventy-third Street.

"This is where I live." I took out my keys.

"Would you have a beer upstairs?" he asked.

I studied Uly for a moment. Suppose he was a multiple murderer. But he taught at the Postgraduate Center.

The Holocaust Studies professor followed me up the four flights to my studio. Thankfully, I had folded up the bed that morning, and covered it with an Indian spread.

"You can sit anywhere," I said, walking into the closet-sized kitchen.

Uly Oppenheim remained standing, rifling through my bookshelves. He pulled out Primo Levi's *Survival in Auschwitz,* turning the pages as if searching for something. He began to read aloud.

"*No human experience is without meaning or unworthy of analysis, and fundamental values, even if they are not positive, can be deduced from this particular world. The Lager was pre-eminently a gigantic biological and social experiment.*"

"Is that supposed to be justification for your book?" I asked, carrying out two St. Pauli Girls, which I carefully placed on my desk, a wooden door set on two file cabinets.

"Aren't you being a little moralistic?"

"The Holocaust is very personal to me."

"Probably to the six million too, not to mention the survivors. To Kraut beer," he toasted me.

"No!" I said, shaking my head as I read the bottle label. "I always assumed this was from Minnesota."

"Hey, I'd drive a Mercedes if I could afford one. What I've got is an old Germy Bug."

I sat down in a wooden chair across from him.

Though older, maybe fifty, he was attractive. I liked his long thick hair with its unruly strands of gray. Eyebrows climbing up his forehead made him look feral, and several hairs brushed the corners of his eyes, which were darkly opaque. But what attracted me was his mind.

"So you were born in Germany?" he asked.

"Yes, a cozy little displaced persons camp near Munich."

"When did you come to the States?" Uly crossed his legs.

That's when I noticed the boots. Tall, black boots that went up his legs, reaching his knees. I found myself staring at them.

"I was, uh, one and a half years old."

"So young." He smiled indulgently at me. "Have you ever been back?"

"No thanks," I said. "That's about the last place I'd ever want to go." Staring at his boots, I thought: *I have a Nazi in my house.*

"It's fascinating, actually. Seeing the place where it all happened."

"I think I'll pass."

"The Poles have turned Auschwitz into a museum. Looks like an Ivy League college. And would you believe they charge fifteen dollars? I refused to pay. Told them my relatives got in for free." He smirked at his own cleverness.

"I don't joke about concentration camps," I said, looking down at his boots again.

"Hey, it's just a fucking factory," he said. "Birkenau is where the actual extermination took place. Did you know it's not even on any of the maps? It's not part of the tourist program. You have to hike across a bridge with no signs. Enormous, too. I climbed one of the watchtowers, looking out in every direction. But there was nothing. No evidence. Just row after row of these horse sheds used as sleeping barracks."

"I don't think I have to hear any more."

He didn't hear me, enthralled with his own story. "It was just these empty fields. It was spring and there were red poppies everywhere—like drops of blood. Nothing like the movies. Then I went back to Auschwitz and stayed at a little hotel that was cheap and clean."

As he took a sip of his beer, I asked, "Why are you telling me this?"

"Because you should know," he answered. "Birkenau has this monument made of stones dedicated to all Nazi victims, *including* the Jews." He emphasized the word. "But especially the poor unfortunate Poles. I tore a page from my notebook and scribbled: 'Look, you fuckers, here I am. I made it. And I'm going to have lots of goddamn Jewish babies.'"

Jewish babies.

"Then I scrolled the paper and stuck it between the stones," he continued.

"Isn't that what Jews do at the Wailing Wall? Leave slips of paper with their prayers."

"You got it."

I stood up. "I haven't any desire to go to Auschwitz."

"We go through our lives thinking of it as a bogeyman. Poland is just a place now—"

"Not for me. It's too real for me. And now it's commercial too. All these Jews going on Heritage Tours to Poland." I shook my head.

"No business like Shoah business," he observed.

"I'm in it too," I told him. "Not by choice. But I can't seem to stop collecting."

I walked over to my black file cabinet. "You see these," I said, pulling out a precariously balanced stack of manila folders. "I have lots more in storage in the basement. My own Holocaust archives."

I opened the top folder, flipping through clipped newspaper articles. "A review of the latest maudlin Holocaust play, *From the Smoking Ashes,* in Greenwich Village," I explained. "An article about an old Nazi living in Queens. Another one in Toronto. A psychological study of the Second Generation sponsored by the National Jewish Mental Health Service."

I picked up the study, beginning to read. "The children of survivors show symptoms that would be expected if they actually lived through the Holocaust. They present a picture of impaired object relations, low self-esteem, narcissistic vulnerability . . . "

"Good, you're working with it," he said, pushing a strand of hair from my face. "That's what we have to do. The only way we can master our demons."

I shook my head. "I wish I could burn the files."

"Do you know what the word *Holocaust* means?"

"Tell me."

"Derives from the Greek *holokaustos*, third century, meaning burnt sacrifice dedicated to God. *Holos* means whole, *kaustos* to burn. Like caustic."

"Burn, baby, burn."

"Burnt whole," he said. "The problem is the word makes it sound like a mystical fire. A sacrifice, instead of the systematic, technocratic murder—"

"I call it the Big H,"

"I prefer Shoah."

"Enough." I drew my hands to my ears. "I really can't listen to this."

"I understand." His Jewish eyes stared into mine.

"Do you?"

"Tell me," he urged.

"My mother's family stayed together in the Czestochowa ghetto for most of the war. On Yom Kippur, they were lined up for Selection. Her mother had tied a white scarf around her head, insisting she wear it. My mother was sent to the death line with her family. Suddenly, a Polish soldier ran along the line, calling, 'Where's the girl with the white scarf?' My mother was dragged to the other line and her life was saved."

"She was lucky."

"But was it the white scarf that saved her life?" I asked him. "My mother thought so. I figured the soldier thought she was too cute to gas."

He took my hands in his. "They all have their stories. But their suffering isn't ours. We didn't go through it. As I've written, the Second Generation has no real experiential content. Just fantasies, overactive, morbid imaginations—"

"What's *your* connection?" I broke in, demanding his CV. "Where were you born?"

"Poland. Actually, the town of Oswiecim."

"Auschwitz!" I exclaimed. "What happened to your family?"

"Who knows? Gone up in smoke, I suppose." He shrugged. "I was hidden during the war. Given to a Catholic family. Raised Catholic. God, I loved baby Jesus. Then I was told I had living family. My mother had survived Bergen-Belsen. She and my stepfather were in some place called Chicago."

"How old were you?"

"Fifteen."

"Is Uly a Hebrew name?"

He laughed. "Ulysses," he said. "Uncircumcised child of anger. My Jewish family wanted nothing to do with Jewish identity."

"And now you teach Holocaust studies," I said, shaking my head. "Why are we talking about this?" I straightened up, stretching my arms.

"Maybe we have to," he said.

"There must be other things to talk about," I insisted.

While the tension between us grew, we studied each other curiously. Offspring of the century's horror show. Freaks of history. Is that what we had in common?

"We're *meshuggeh* people," I quoted him.

"But passionate," he added, putting his arms around my waist. "Do your parents receive *wiedergutmacht*?" He drew me near.

"German reparations payments?"

He nodded. "Survivor *gelt*."

"Survivor guilt," I said. "Of course."

"This one is for us." He kissed me on the lips suddenly. I pulled back for a moment, probing his eyes, so dark, unknowable.

"I find myself very attracted to you," he said softly. "Even if you are a refugee."

"And what are you?" I asked. "Son of the D.A.R.?"

"I want you, Zoe."

"Whoa! Hold on a minute." I pulled back, looking at him. "You work kind of fast, don't you?"

"You want me too, you sexy Polish Jewess." He pulled me to him, grabbing a hunk of my hair. "You with your beautiful Zivia Lubetkin hair."

"Who's that?"

"She fought the hell out of the Nazis in the Warsaw ghetto. Killed, naturally." He kissed me lightly on the mouth. "I've only seen pictures of her, but she had your wild hair." He kissed me again. "Zosha—"

"Zoe," I corrected him.

"You're Zosha," he said, gently combing my hair with his fingers.

Being so close to him, I heard his breathing. Short, quickening. I could feel his body quiver.

"That's what my mother calls me," I muttered.

"If you tell me you love someone and he loves you, I'll leave you alone, Zosha."

"We just met tonight. You don't know—"

"We've known each other a long time," he whispered in my ear.

"I don't believe that."

He kissed me gently.

"Do you have someone—?" I began as he kissed my neck. I put my arms around his waist. For several moments, we moved very slowly to an ancient song.

The telephone rang, startling both of us. I reached out. "Don't pick it up," he pleaded. Second ring. Third. Fourth.

"I have to!" I cried, freeing myself from his hold.

"Oh, hi." I groaned softly. "Yes, I'm right here. I can't talk right now. It's not a good time, Mom. Because I'm not alone. Yes, someone's here. You don't know the person. Yes, it's a man. No. I won't tell you his name." I rolled my eyes at Uly. "Mom! I have to go. I'll call you tomorrow. Please. Okay, I promise. I'm hanging up. Yes, Mom. I'll double-lock the door after he leaves."

I hung up the receiver, sighing deeply as I sat down on the couch. "Speaking of—" I shook my head.

"Aren't you a little old to have your mother calling at this hour?" he asked.

"She doesn't think so. What can I say? She worries about me because I live alone."

"All survivors are overprotective," he said. "Where were we?" He approached me.

"The D.A.R."

"And I was trying to seduce you." He ran his fingers under my sweater.

I pulled away from him. "Can't we just talk?"

"Isn't that what we've been doing for hours?" He looked down at his watch. "It's eleven o'clock."

"Is there a time limit?"

"I should probably go," he said, turning impatient. "It's getting late."

"No, don't, Uly," I said. "Not yet. I'll be right back."

In the confessional of the bathroom mirror, I studied my face. What the hell was I doing? Did I really want to sleep with him tonight? I had told myself that I wasn't going to do that anymore.

The Liz Taylor eyes were mussed with black makeup, my lipstick clownish. Sure, I felt drawn to him. He was an attractive man. Still. I splashed water over my face and hands. The Holocaust professor waited for me.

When I returned, Uly reclined on the couch. He had taken off his black boots, which stood up straight, invisible legs inside them.

As I sat down on the couch, I couldn't take my eyes off his boots. I imagined an SS officer inside them, wearing a long coat, a swastika armband on his sleeve. Uly pulled me to him, starting to kiss me again.

I drew away from him. "Why do you wear those boots?"

He looked perplexed. "You don't like them?"

"They're Nazi boots."

"Zoe," he said softly, trying to placate me. "I bought them at Florsheim's on Broadway. A store owned by Jews," he added in his defense. "On sale."

I picked them up. Heavy. The black leather hard. I dropped the boots behind the arm of the couch, out of sight.

"Why don't we take off our clothes?" he suggested. "Be naked together. *Mano a mano*."

"I have a little bit of grass," I offered, stalling for time.

"Oh." His eyes twinkled. "Let's stoke it up."

I went into one of my file cabinets, pulling out a plastic baggie. "Can you roll?" I asked.

"Can I roll? You bet I can." He threw himself into his task. Starting with an extra-large Bambu rolling paper, he rolled it into a perfect cylinder.

"*Voilà!* Now we just need a flame."

"Right here." I pulled a lighter from the baggie.

We sat comfortably next to each other on the couch. He placed the joint in my mouth, held it while I inhaled, and then I put it in his mouth. Back and forth.

"Mmmm . . . " He lay his head back on the couch. "I don't know about you, but I got buzzed."

I took another puff. "Me too."

"C'm'ere." He pulled me to him.

"Do you want to hear some music? I've got this great reissue of Miles Davis's *Kind of*—"

He stood up, loosening his tie, gray silk with a red stripe down its center. "Let's just lie together. Nothing will happen you don't want to happen. I promise, Zosha."

"I'm not ready." I paused. "I feel too ambivalent."

"This is ridiculous," he said angrily. He pulled his tie

off, rolling it up like a snake in his hand. "It's time for me to split." He reached over the bolster for his boots.

"No!" I implored. "Couldn't you just stay for a few more minutes? Tell me to take my clothes off—again," I whispered.

"Take *my* clothes off," Uly ordered.

I moved over to his lap, opening the buttons of his shirt. He placed my hand so I could feel his hardness straining against the fabric of his pants.

At that moment, I felt my power. I could do what I wanted with him. It was a delicious thought: how much he needed me. I could withdraw my hand. I could tell him to go to hell. I could, but I didn't. He could kill me. I placed myself squarely on top of him, grinding into his hardness.

"Zosha," he sighed.

That was the clincher. I relaxed into his arms, letting him take off my sweater. "Let's get rid of these too." My leather skirt. He nearly ripped my lace panties.

"Uly—"

"No talk," he said, reaching over to pick up his tie from the floor. He slipped it around my neck.

We began to kiss again. Light, flirty kisses. Tongues teasing. Probing. Retreating.

Slowly, serpentine, he draped his tie around the back of my neck, swirling it like a sash. Then he ran it down my back, over my bare buttocks. Starting over again, my neck, my back, beginning to run his tie between my legs, then withdrawing.

"Does it excite you?" he asked.

"Yes," I whispered, trying to grab the tie with my thighs, holding it there. He pulled it. I started to grind as he lashed the tie between my thighs.

"I love the way you move your ass," he muttered.

Grabbing the ends, he began to whip the tie over me. Back and forth. Sawing me in half like a magician. Oh, the sensation of the rope.

"You don't like that much, do you?"

"Don't stop."

He was the master. *Ubermensch.* Superman. So powerful. It was 1942. I was a prisoner. Jew. Whore. The ends swished against my thighs. I clasped the tie between my legs. He pulled it tighter, caressing me softly. I pressed his hands hard against my breasts.

"Is that what you want?"

"*Tak*," I answered him in Polish. Yes.

He turned me over, the tie wrapped between my legs.

"Don't stop," I repeated breathlessly.

He had selected me from the others. If I made him love me, he'd take me through the war. I would survive. He could give me Jewish babies.

Uly ran his tongue back and forth. Now his fingers reached inside to zero in on my hardness. I pressed against his finger, tongue, mashing against him as I started to come.

He climbed behind me. "I've got something for you, my little refugee," he whispered. "This comes all the way from Oswiecim."

He entered me slowly. His body tensed as he started his pounding, which was hard and fast, pounding against me.

Afterward, as he slept next to me, I watched him. My rescuer! He had known me as an outsider could never know me. Once he opened his eyes, still asleep. *My blood brother.* I dozed for several hours, his leg flanking mine.

It was a familiar dream. The locks were forced, the door to my apartment opening slowly. I could see the silhouette of a man, stalking across the studio. As he approached my bed, I could see a knife in his hand. I was about to scream. That's when I woke up. The bed was empty next to me.

"Uly," I called in the dark.

"I'm right here."

My eyes adjusted, seeing his figure bent over.

"What's the matter?" I asked.

"I've got to go."

I switched on the reading light, glancing at the clock. Two-thirty. "Why are you leaving?"

He reached to pick up his tie. *My tie.* I longed to keep it as a memento.

"I've got to go." He coiled the tie, dropping it into his jacket pocket.

"Why?" I sat up.

"Because I have to get up early tomorrow. Actually, in a few hours."

"There's an alarm." I climbed out of bed. "Don't go yet."

He sat down on the bed, pulling on his boot. "Zoe, did you see my other boot?"

"I don't get it." I sat down next to him, pulling a T-shirt over my nakedness. "Why do you have to leave? It's not as if you live with someone."

He nodded ruefully. "I thought you knew." He bent over to reach his other boot under the bed. He looked up at me. "Everyone knows it. I did think you were aware of Maria—"

"Maria?"

"She converted, and is actually more religious than me," he said. "She lights candles on Friday night."

"Does your girlfriend know about—this?"

"No, of course not." He looked grimly at me. "I'm sorry, Zoe. I thought you knew. She's my wife."

"Why don't you wear a fucking ring!"

"We don't have that kind of marriage," he began.

That's when I looked down at the despised black boots. How could I have given myself to this Nazi, this married Nazi Jew! I kicked one of the boots with my bare foot, bruising my big toe.

"Zoe, you're a terrific woman," he continued. "You're young, so you don't know that yet."

"I get it," I said, waking from my dream. "I'm the Jewish girl you screw after your Holocaust lecture."

"Look, I told you, I'm attracted to you."

"Yes, I know. My Zivia Lubetkin hair. "

"And you're attracted to me." He reached out to hold me.

"Uh-uh." I pulled away from him.

"Grow up, Zoe," he said, then added, "Does it really matter? I have a long marriage. We're more roommates than anything. We have no children. Actually, it's quite sad."

I was taken aback for a moment. What about the Jewish babies?

"Look, I'm not the prick you think I am. Have you read my book?"

I shook my head.

He picked up his briefcase, snapped it open, pulling out *Our Bodies, Not Our Souls.*

He handed me his book, then took it back. "Wait, I want to write something." Sitting down on the edge of the bed, he bent down, his thick hair falling over his forehead. He looked up at me momentarily, pushed the hair from his face, then began to write. "Here."

I turned to the title page. *"Welcome to the club. Uly Oppenheim."*

"What club is that?" I asked, paging to the table of contents. "You mean like Gertrud F. and Eva Z.?"

"We're the ones left holding the bag," he said gravely.

I slammed the book shut, returning it to him. "Not me," I said, shaking my head. "Not my club. This was just temporary insanity."

I stepped over my black leather skirt, red sweater, my panties splayed grotesquely.

"No matter what you do, you're stuck with the Holocaust. So is the rest of the world. But you, Zosha, have a special task."

"Is this supposed to be some sort of lesson from the Holocaust professor?"

"You're a smart kid." He patted me on the ass. "You know those files of yours—" He raised those hairy brows of his. "Write something."

I met his stare. "What makes you think I haven't?"

TRIPTYCH

The phone rang. No one. I dropped the receiver, threw the blanket over my head. Still ringing! I picked up and heard a dial tone.

I tumbled out of bed, ran into the kitchen, and pressed the downstairs TALK button. "Who is it?" I called.

"Zosha," the garbled voice screeched. "Your father and me are standing already here ten minutes. Open up already!"

Saturday morning. *How can they do this to me?* I buzzed them into the building, then raced into the bathroom.

Dammit! I ran cold water over my face. *What do they want?* I looked in the mirror. Last night's mascara was smudged around my eyes like bruises.

My mother was panting as she climbed the final steps,

a shopping bag clutched in her hand. She stopped to catch her breath, then said, "I can't see why you don't have an elevator like a human being."

My mother's hair, dyed dull beige like all of her cronies', was teased in a bouffant with wings. She wore a two-piece lavender ensemble she'd sewn herself, turquoise beads and earrings, pale stockings, heels.

I looked down at myself, standing there barefoot and wild-haired, my ancient chenille robe falling apart.

Heniek followed flatfootedly behind. In contrast to my mother's getup, he looked like a Ben Shahn drawing of a working man in American clothes. A blunt hat with a feather covered his head as he bent over, checking his watch with a jagged flick of his wrist.

"Couldn't you at least call first?" I finally said, tying the frayed belt of my bathrobe.

"What, are we strangers?" Genia demanded. She leaned toward me, trying to push a stray hair out of my eyes.

"That's not the point," I snapped, throwing my mother's hand off. What if I was with someone? They had no respect for my privacy. An obscene, ungrateful word. "Normal people call before they burst in on you first thing in the morning," I insisted.

"Pish, posh," Genia answered. "You're such a fancy lady we have to make an appointment?"

They stood in the hallway outside my apartment, my family, bathed in acid green lighting.

"So we can come in?" Genia said finally. "Here." She passed me the heavy shopping bag.

"What's this?" I asked.

"Wait," she said. "First I go to the toilet."

Genia never entered a place without rushing to the bathroom. Once she had been forced to pee in the *pushka*, and then only when the women guards in the camp gave her permission. Now Genia knew where the ladies rooms were in every major department store as well as hotel and restaurant in the city.

Heniek sat on the couch, picked up a magazine, then a book, *Our Bodies, Not Our Souls* by Uly Oppenheim, Ph.D. The cover was a real grabber with its vivid red letters and the black garter with a swastika.

"What's this?" he asked, beginning to leaf through the pages. My father read everything written about the war.

"I met the author. He gave me a copy," I answered. "It's about brothels in the camps."

"It's not a lie," he said. "Such things happened. Believe me, I saw much worse than that."

"You have the day off?" I asked, attempting the impossible: to engage my father in a conversation.

He didn't hear, flipping the pages.

"You're not working?" I repeated.

Without looking up, he said, "You want me to go?"

"Of course not," I said pleasantly. "Do you want tea, Dad?"

"Don't bother."

"It's no bother." I filled the kettle.

"I don't want nothing."

"Look, I'm making it anyway. If you want something . . . "

"I told you, I won't touch it. If you give it to me, I'll spit it out!" he responded. "Let me read."

I watched from across the room, trying to make sense of this totally incomprehensible stranger. How he burrowed himself into books like an animal in its hole. I rarely saw him without something in his hand, a newspaper, *Time* magazine, a book about the Holocaust.

"Now I have to change my shoes," Genia declared, sitting down to remove her pumps. "These hurt like hell."

I had read somewhere that shoes were crucial for surviving. Once your shoes went, you couldn't walk anymore. My father had wrapped newspapers around his feet during the war when he had to march for hours in the snow . . .

Genia reached into the shopping bag and took out a housecoat and a pair of gold fake leather slippers. "Ach, my feet burn." As she eased the first slipper onto her foot, she sighed. "Only in slippers are my feet happy."

Then she slowly removed the ensemble she faced the world in, the Americans. Standing in her full slip, she buttoned her daisy-patterned housecoat.

"Would you like tea, Mom?"

"No, I had already."

"Nothing?"

"Maybe a piece of bread?" She removed several plastic containers from the bag.

Genia always brought food. Just in case some disaster befell them. Besides, she was convinced I was starving, living by myself with no food in my refrigerator.

"I brought you *krupnik* for two times, remember to take off the fat with a spoon, and a little *cholent*. I made it last week for company but saved some for you."

"Thanks."

I placed a loaf of black bread on a wooden board with a sharp knife. "Do you want jam or cheese?"

"Heniek," Genia called, "Look what your daughter put out for us. Such a spread."

"I don't want nothing," he repeated.

"Well, I'll have a cup of coffee anyway," I declared, pouring the boiling water through a filter. I stared down, watching the coffee solidify inside the white cone.

As my mother sliced the black bread, she said, "You know, the Russians gave Daddy two loaves of black bread a day. After the war, he was only forty-seven kilos. In four months—" She stopped and looked at me. "Why are you so sour, daughter of mine?"

"Because I told you I want you to call before you come."

"You used to be such a happy child."

"I need to take a shower."

"What about your coffee?"

"I'll take it with me."

"Okay, I'll clean up." She ran her finger over the windowsill. "Look how much dust you have."

"No!" I screamed. Then gentler. "Please, don't."

"You can't just take a cloth and wipe the surface? You should be ashamed."

"Mom, why do you have to do this to me?" I asked.

"What am I doing? That I don't want you to live like this for the rest of your life?"

I didn't want to get into it, but I couldn't help myself.

"What's wrong with the way I live?" I demanded.

"Alone?"

"Not always."

She raised her right eyebrow, then said, "Like a dog. An orphan lives better." Then her tone turned solicitous. "Not always? So . . . " she clucked. "Is there someone, Zosha, in your life . . . "

I didn't answer.

"A nice Jewish man," she said, "with a good job—"

"Get off it, Mom!"

"Okay, kill me. I worry for you. I want you should have a good life."

"I have a good life," I answered.

"Family life is everything for a woman."

I said nothing, rolling my eyes.

"Children are—what can I say? Everything." She looked seriously into my eyes. "*Nu*, Zosha?"

"I'm not ready yet," I answered.

Genia's voice turned sharp, like a barbed instrument. "How long you will wait? Till your eggs dry up and rot?"

"I'm taking my shower."

My father did not look up from *Our Bodies, Not Our Souls* as I walked past him. With relief, I locked the bathroom door behind me. Slowly, I stripped.

I turned on the hot water. It scalded my skin. I didn't want to move. *Heal me, I am broken.* I started to cry.

The righteous jets of water massaged my back and neck. I wished I could stand still forever, silver rivulets of water running over my body. Free of them and their painful history.

My father was still reading when I walked past him, wrapped in my robe. He did not look up. In my bedroom, I found my mother standing over my desk.

I rushed in. "What are you doing? You know I don't want you looking at things on my desk."

This time I caught her red-handed, holding a typed page from my manuscript. I tried to grab it from her. "Mom—!"

"What is it?" Genia asked.

"Something I'm working on."

"So many pages," she muttered. "Like a book."

I reached for the sheet in her hand. "Mother—"

"Is it about us?" she asked shrewdly.

"I don't talk about it," I said, grabbing the sheet.

"You know how often I've told you to write for *Martyrdom and Remembrance*. They publish many Second

Generation. Manya's daughter, Eleanor, wrote such a touching poem. It made me cry!"

"I'm not interested in *Martyrdom*."

"Our good friend, Bolek, is the editor, and he always asks about you. I'm sure he would be interested in your poems."

"I'm still not interested in *Martyrdom*."

I looked down. Where I had grabbed the sheet of paper from my mother, a jagged diagonal rip formed. I took a deep breath.

"First, you burst in on me when I'm sleeping. While I'm in the bathroom, you go through my stuff. What's wrong with you?"

"You're right. You're always right," she admitted. "I shouldn't look at your things, but—" She paused for a moment. "We came to talk to you about something."

"Oh." I stopped in my tracks. "What's wrong?"

"Your father and I are going to Poland," she declared gravely.

"No!" I gasped. "When?"

"Next month. For two weeks."

"I can't believe it," I said, shaking my head.

"I couldn't sleep all night," my mother muttered.

"I just can't understand why," I responded. "You've always hated the Poles. You said they were worse than the Germans, that they were still killing Jews after the war, that you would never go back—"

"It's time," she said. "We need to see. We have to do it, that's all."

I sat down on my bed, stunned. "I still can't believe it. Are you going by yourselves?"

"Oh no, Stella Brumstein and Beniek are going, and Vatska and Nusen, some others from the Czestochowa Society you don't know."

"It's the fiftieth anniversary of Warsaw Uprising," my father shouted from the living room.

"I should go with you," I said.

"Why?" my mother asked.

"Because I need to see it too," I answered.

"It's better not," she said, shaking her head firmly.

"Why?" I demanded, staring at her. "You're going to protect me—now?"

"It's not for you to go," she insisted. "You're an American."

"But you've told me all about the war."

"Maybe I told you too much," she said, shaking her head.

"I should see Poland for myself," I insisted.

"It's not there, Zosh."

"Warsaw?"

"They destroyed everything. We almost didn't get out after the war. The Poles didn't have enough blood. We had to escape like criminals to Berlin." She paused, looking sadly at me.

"You're our daughter, so you heard things. You had no *bubbe*, no granny to sit on her lap, to hear good stories," she continued. "I talked too much. I didn't have my mother to help me, to teach me things."

"I need to know where we come from," I insisted. "Who we are. Who I am," I added softly.

"But you don't need to go there," she asserted. "Go to Israel. Maybe there you'll meet a *sabra*."

"If that's what I want, I'll call Shalom Moving," I answered.

"Always a wisecrack. Like when you went to school. Heniek," she now cried, "come and talk to her."

He looked up. "What do you want me to say?" he asked. "She'll do what she wants. She always did."

"What did I do?" I asked.

Slowly, he stood up. Walking into the bedroom, he looked around suspiciously, his eyes fixing on the double bed. He stared underneath the bed as if he might spot a lover crawling out on all fours.

"Your mother worries about you," he began uncomfortably, as if he were once again the reluctant spanker, and I the *paskudnyak* evil girl.

"She worries about everything," I responded.

"What, would you like parents who don't care what you do?"

"No," I admitted. "But there's nothing to worry about."

"I don't know why you made me come, Genia," he groaned. "I've got to go to work."

"Your important work will be there in a few minutes. Talk your daughter," she insisted.

He stood there, glowering. Finally, he said, "So you want to go with us?"

I nodded. "I do."

"You know what's in Poland? Nothing," he spat the word. "Nothing!"

"Why are you going?" I asked.

"Because we have to."

"I do too, Dad."

"You? Don't be ridiculous!" he scoffed.

"It's part of me too," I insisted.

"You don't know nothing about it!" His voice was getting louder.

"That's not true. I've read books, seen movies. I know I wasn't there, but—"

"You should only thank God you weren't there!" he yelled.

"Why are you screaming at me?"

"Talk like a human being to her," Genia said softly.

"Do you think I want to go back?" he asked. "But your mother, she gets these ideas."

"Don't worry," I said angrily, "I'll pay for myself."

"*Boje, boje.* God, god," he sighed loudly. "It isn't enough that we went through it? Now you want to go? Why?" he demanded. "Why?"

"So I'll understand."

"Understand what?" he asked. "Auschwitz?"

"It's part of me too. It's something I've imagined in great detail!" I cried out. "I've been there. Don't you understand?"

He shook his head sadly. "If you want me to lie to you, I'll say I understand. I don't understand! You've had everything."

I turned to my mother. "Is anyone living in Warsaw?" I asked her, trying another tack.

"Not our family," Genia answered.

"Not a single distant relative?"

Genia shook her head.

"Nobody from Daddy's side?"

"You've met my cousin, Jack, on Grand Concourse," Genia said quietly. "Daddy has Uncle Miecho in Israel and his family—"

"Just a minute," I said, taking a yellow pad from my desk. "I don't even know the names. I want to make a family tree."

"A tree!" Heniek laughed bitterly. "Without branches or leaves."

"We're not in touch," Genia added.

"I don't care. I just want to be able to see the names. To know that these people once existed. I don't even know their names," I told my father.

"What does it matter?" he demanded. "It's not real." Heniek grabbed the pad, trying to tear it in half. "Names! They're all dead! I don't know even why we have to go."

"Don't start, Heniek! I want to see what's there. My father owned property. People say some of the buildings still stand."

"There's nothing left. Just a giant cemetery for Jews. And even those stones are broken. Used for doorstops." He started to walk to the door. "*Choleras,* all of them!"

"Heniek, just a minute." She ran after him.

"The meter will run out," he said. "You want to pay fifty dollars?"

"So stick a quarter in," she said.

"I have to go." He held the book under his arm. "I'll give you this back next week."

"Pick me up with the car before you go home," Genia called after Heniek.

The door slammed behind him.

I opened the door, watching my father as he stomped down the stairs. The steel stairwell vibrated with rage. It was as if something terrible had happened. But what? And why was it my fault?

He turned to look up the stairwell at me for a moment, then continued walking down the steps.

I almost said—something. I don't know what. Then, I called after him. "Daddy!"

He stopped, squinting up to see me.

I didn't know what to say. "Dad?"

He stood still for several seconds. When he turned his face toward me, I saw a slight smile, or at least, I thought I did. For a moment, he resembled a younger, cockier man. Then he shook his head. "Ach, Zosha." He sighed joylessly.

/ / /

I shut the door. Genia approached me. "It's just too painful for him. He tries, but he just can't talk about some things."

"He can't stand me," I said.

"Don't be stupid," she said sharply. "Your father loves you. Why do you think he works so hard?"

"But why does he scream at me like that?"

"That's the way he is. It doesn't mean nothing."

"To me it does."

"Don't you know your father yet? After all these years. He's a good man, Zosh, who works too hard. But does he love you? How can you even ask?"

"What does he think of my writing?"

"What's to think? You always wrote. He doesn't read such things like poetry. Do you understand?" she asked me.

I shrugged.

"But you have a right to know," she declared, picking up the yellow pad. "I know some of the names. Let's make the tree."

"It was a stupid idea," I said ruefully. "Dad's right. What does it matter? Everyone's dead."

"They weren't born dead, Zosha," she said, beginning to sketch an egg-shaped outline. "Warsaw was a big city before the war. This is where we lived, before they forced us out." She was drawing a map of her past life in Poland.

"Marszalkowska was the main street with many fancy shops." She filled in street names on the map. "We lived on the next street, Mokotowska Number Seven, in a building next to door of a hat store. I remember the name. Zygmund Kapelusz. A Jew. He was killed, of course, but his house still stood after the war. So did ours. Maybe still."

She drew two tiny boxes. "Here was Ziemanska and Kapulski cafes where musicians played. The church Anna Maria on Chlodna Number Ten." She drew a cross on the map. "We used to play Burn the Church. Even before the war, we hated the Poles. All the boys would open the buttons of their pants and pee at a can or box in the courtyard. They wouldn't let me play. But once they did. I was so excited. They told me to stand in the center and close my eyes." She started to giggle. "Suddenly all of them were peeing on me."

"Oh, no!" I exclaimed. "What did you do?"

"I ran home and my mother cleaned me up."

We both laughed. My mother's laugh girlish, her fingers still hiding her teeth, which had long ago been fixed.

"Mom, do you know why you survived?" I asked.

She shook her head. "Lot of people were better people than me, smarter, and still they died. No one knows why."

"How did you begin to live?" I asked. "After everything that happened—"

"Such a question. I don't know. Life makes you live."

"Was it difficult?"

"It just happened," she said. "One whole day passes and you don't think of nothing. Then you do. It's not so good. It puts you in bad mood. So you don't think about it. You think about something else and you're careful not to think of anything. You make new friends, you buy clothing, you keep busy."

"Did you ever think not to bring children into such a world?"

"Never," she answered. "They killed us, not our seed." Then she looked at me. "You were our greatest pleasure."

My eyes welled up. "Mom—" I said hoarsely, reaching out to touch her arm.

"I never meant to pass it on to you." She clutched my hand, stroking it. "You were my miracle. Without no scars. When you were born, your father said, 'This is worth more than a million American dollars.'"

"He really said that?" I asked.

She nodded.

"I have an idea, Zosha," she said suddenly. "Let's go shopping."

"Now?"

"To that store on Broadway. What's it called? Job's Odd Lot?"

"You mean, Odd Job Lot?"

She nodded eagerly.

"What about Dad? Didn't you ask him to pick you up from here?"

"He won't come so fast," she said.

"But they only have junk, Mom."

"What's junk to one person can be diamonds to someone else."

Other mothers took their daughters to Lord & Taylor. My mother examined plastic alarm clocks, fiesta-colored napkin rings, bedsheet seconds, discontinued Water Piks, electric curlers, and Israeli pantyhose. I followed behind her, strangely comforted.

I had spent a lifetime of Saturdays crawling with my mother through the aisles of Lane's, Klein's, and the street bazaar of Fourteenth Street, as colorful and glittery as anything Cairo could offer.

Now I dragged behind her as she stalked the aisles like a spy, filling her wire basket. "Look at this!" she cried out, picking up a pair of picture frames inlaid with iridescent mother-of-pearl butterflies. "These would look nice in your apartment."

I shook my head.

"Knickknacks make a place friendlier."

"No thanks."

"Only two ninety-nine," she exulted. "On Fifth Avenue, I saw exactly the same picture frames for ten dollars each. It'll look great in the bedroom, above the bed." She tried to put the frames in her basket.

I removed them firmly. "I don't have any wall space."

She stuck them back into the basket, covering it with her arm so I couldn't reach them. She was fierce.

Continuing down the aisle, Genia studied a blue cardigan, put it down, swinging the hangers as she searched.

"I could use this in Poland," she said, holding up a white knit sweater with small pearl buttons. "Sometimes it's very cold at night."

Her face was younger, prettier as she buttoned the white cardigan. "How does it look on me, Zosha?" she asked dreamily.

There was no messiah. Only the *metziah*. A bargain.

THIEVES

Why should I feel a thief? Genia hangs up her coat in Zosha's closet, straightening out a tweed blazer slipping off a bent wire hanger. She enters the kitchen, puts on the yellow rubber gloves she has brought, begins to wash dishes. She knows Zosha isn't happy when she lets herself into her apartment. But she doesn't mind to find the place clean and neat, like only her mother can do it.

For several moments, Genia stands motionless in her daughter's small apartment. "Zosha, how do you live?" she says aloud. "With nothing. A few books and records. Your used clothes from thrift shops. Why can't you buy decent things?" Then she begins to scrub a frying pan caked with egg.

Her tiny kitchen with peeling white paint. Everything quiet except the hum of the refrigerator. Too quiet. Only the pilot light is alive. No potholders, colorful dish towels, calendars, recipes. Knickknacks make a place friendlier. Nothing but glasses clear as ice, mugs hanging from copper hooks. And the Rosenthal china teapot she gave her from Landsberg. Genia picks it up and notices a thin crack. Water bleeds from the cut as she fills it.

"*Kalecka*," she mutters. Clumsy one. Always everything breaks with her. *Kalecka*, always falling, hurting herself. Wherever she stepped, glass flew in the air, nails cut her, her knees black with cracking scabs and iodine.

Genia begins her slow walk around the apartment.

Who is this stranger with her books everywhere? Important friends, editors, she calls them. The machine that mocks her. "Hi, it's Zoe. Glad you called but I'm not here. If you leave your name and—" Never. She hangs up, will not talk to a machine. Her name is Zosha Hanna, after both of their mothers. A stranger, her daughter.

Genia's eyes fall on the portrait of Zosha, the one the German photographer took. "*Ya pamientam*. I remember. We were famous. Everyone stopped to look at her in the photo shop window in Landsberg. People said she could be Elizabeth Taylor's sister. It took your breath away. Her eyes so blue, her perfect mouth. Zosha is still good-looking, but who knows what she does, who she goes out with?"

When we look at each other, does she remember? How we lay in rapture. I cradled her in my arms, our eyes never leaving each other. She started to cry. I tickled her tummy, softer than peaches, made sounds so she'd giggle. Her laugh, a surprise, the tinkle of high-strung chimes, her little mouth too small for a spoon.

I don't even know how I knew to make such sounds. I taught her to see colors, naming each one so she'd know. The red wool of her doll's hair, and I sewed a special dress, yellow with blue stars. Like the mittens I knitted for Jesse—before they were taken away. Yellow wool with tiny blue knots. Zosha's doll's eyes opened and closed. *A-leep*, Zosha's first American word.

Genia walks into the other room with her desk and the big bed. Too big for one person. Why three pillows? The bedspread she sewed from curtains of Zosha's old room, black roses on white velour. Clean sheets. Her closet full of jeans and sweaters thrown together like a *shlump*, wrinkled.

Genia suspects that she has lovers, but this is something she cannot bear to think about. How they use her daughter for their pleasure. And does she burn for them, her body contorting to allow their invasion?

As she folds Zosha's sweaters, placing them in one stack and jeans in another, she argues, "Zosha, I don't see why you had to leave. Everything was perfect—" Her fingers pluck each hanger with the aplomb of a harpist. She pulls out one of the dresses. Blue gray with small circles on the hem. Genia holds it in her arms, dipping at the waist to a Strauss waltz.

Will she ever know what it's like to have such a child? Everytime I looked at her, I felt happy. Like a contessa, she seemed, when Zosha wore it Yom Hashoah. I lit a candle for all of them, especially my Jesse. Her black hair swelling in waves at the shoulders. The long tapered legs of Zosha, which are not mine, nor her gift for words. They were always like from a book, so fine, better even than born Americans. And to see Zosha's name on the masthead in an American magazine. And her own maiden name too! I'm famous! Genia smiles wickedly.

"I don't know the words you know, college graduate. I sound funny, I know, your *matka*, the greenhorn . . . "

A flowered woolen scarf covers Zosha's electric typewriter. Genia lifts it, running her fingers over the keys. If only she could write her stories. So they'd know. Where she comes from, not a *shtetl,* their beautiful house on Mokotowska, her family, educated and cultured, not like the others from *shtetls,* her mother's uncle Lolek, a doctor.

Zosha's large dictionary, golden letters in black shiny arches on the edge. *Roget's Thesaurus.* What's that? Genia opens it, glancing at a random page: "78-80 Abstract Relations. Inclusion. Generality. Specialty." She shuts it hastily. *The Oxford Dictionary of Quotations.* An ashtray. Genia empties the butts into a wicker basket. There are two empty beer cans and crumpled sheets of paper.

She reaches inside for one of the sheets. Straightening it out, she struggles to make out her daughter's handwriting. The crossing out. Words on top of words. She pulls another sheet from the basket. The same thing, a few different words. Another sheet with typing. The same thing. Why does she write it so many times? Slowly, lips moving, Genia begins to read the scrawled page. A poem! What her Zosha wrote.

> *I haven't seen it,*
> *but I know it's luminescent,*
> *not like moonlight, but teeth*
> *without gold fillings, fingernail moons.*
>
> *It was hidden in a hole*
> *in the wall of their basement.*
> *The house lasted the war.*
> *My mother's father's cigarette case.*
>
> *She returned to the house,*
> *the hole, and found her mother's diamond ring,*

the family's savings in a cup,
the cigarette case of her father.

She spent the silver coins on a fling.
She made the diamond ring mine,
and to her uncle, who saved her life,
she gave her father's cigarette case.

He stopped smoking in his sixtieth year
and hid the cigarette case in a safe place.
His wife wrote it into her will
to be left for her sister's children.

My mother heard her father's voice:
"Genia, Genusha, my little Genska,
give to yourself, give to yourself
as I wish I could have given to you."

She wrote a letter to her uncle,
asking for her father's cigarette case.
It arrived soon afterwards, without a fuss,
my mother's father's cigarette case.

She's crying, I know it,
into her father's cigarette case.
Salt is spilling on the linoleum!
My mother lies down in the water

Floating to where her mother waits.
Momma is wearing her seal-collared coat.
Tata, her father, stands next to her.
And Jesse waves, hands warm in his mittens.

Genia is breathless when she finishes. It means so much that Zosha takes an interest. Many of her friends' children don't even listen to the stories, but her Zosha always wanted to know everything. And Genia told her as much as she thought was right.

But she asked so many questions. How did your mother die? How did your father die? Did your brother cry? Did they torture you? Did they torture Daddy? Did you have any boyfriend before Daddy?

There are several school notebooks on Zosha's desk. What a good student she was. An honor student. Genia opens one. Full of her daughter's jagged black handwriting. Who can read it? Hieroglyphs! She narrows her eyes but is unable to decipher the words.

Genia opens a drawer in Zosha's desk. Pens, pencils, paper clips. What she uses. The file drawer sticks, but Genia tugs at it. Inside, hidden under papers and folders, she finds a stack of typed sheets.

As she reads the first page, her breath grows short, her heart pounding. *Like a real book from the library.* If Zosha writes a bestseller, Heniek and me will be immoral—forever.

She sits down on Zosha's bed and begins to read. At first, it is difficult. So many thoughts and feelings rush through her. So fast.

I am named Zosha Hanna, after both of my parents' murdered mothers. I spent my first year with hundreds of Jewish refugees, orphans of large families and communities, in the American Zone of the Displaced Persons camp in Landsberg, Germany. Polish and Yiddish swelled the air.

We came to America. I forgot my Polish. I was an American girl with no accent. I had friends, my own life, which I longed to grow into like a pair of oversize shoes. When I left home, I intended to create a self that had nothing to do with my parents' past. But I wanted to be a writer. A dangerous vocation.

It is our way to tell tales, bug-eyed people of the Book. We become writers and therapists because we believe in the power of storytelling. As if the right arrangement of words could release us.

As a child, my parents' stories held me with the power of prehistoric myth. Such stories. Lives saved by split-second decisions, coincidences that strained credibility, amazing reversals. One of my parents' friends had been in the showers when the gas failed and her execution was postponed. Another had been dropped in a mass grave, pretended to be dead, and climbed out in the dark.

Then there were the unlucky ones, the man who lit a cigarette and was shot, the young mother who was taken away, leaving behind her little boy, Izo. My mother and several women in the camp hid him in a hole in the wall. Somehow he knew not to cry. They watched fearfully as Izo grew larger, knowing he would soon be discovered. One day they returned from work and he was gone.

"Izo!" Genia whispers his name. "*Ya pamietam.* I remember."

I don't ever remember not knowing. I believe I sucked the knowledge in my mother's milk. It gave me a secret inner life that was as voluptuous as it was tortured.

Then I saw my first footage of the camps. Maybe I was eight. I had walked in as my parents sat in front of our black-and-white Westinghouse television. I watched hundreds of naked bodies, more bone than flesh, dumped in the bottom of a huge cavity. The skeletons dropped like debris into the mass grave. I observed close-ups of faces with vacant, wide-eyed stares. I stood there as my mother wept. My father peered intently at the television set as if he might recognize someone he knew. Neither noticed me.

"No. It's not true," Genia argues. "I always noticed you."

We call ourselves 2Gs. Group shorthand for Second Generation, the survivors' children. We have organizations with names like the Generation After, support groups and kinship meetings, well-attended conferences in the States and Israel. There is even a group, One to One, which joins children of Holocaust survivors with children of Nazis.

While the survivors seem to have the ability to go on with their lives—the bar mitzvahs and weddings of their children are huge, festive affirmations of life—it is their children who spend much of their time, not to mention money, talking to Ph.D.'s, and MSWs. In unaccented, well-reasoned English, we speak of anger, guilt, trying to separate ourselves from our parents and their Holocaust past. Secretly, we believe that nothing we can ever do will be as important as our parents' suffering.

Enough! Genia wants to stop but sits there like a prisoner, reading. The words jumping off the pages. Her daughter's words, picking at her like sharp-beaked birds.

There is a hierarchy of suffering. Treblinka survivors feel superior to the ones who were in Terezin—summer camp in comparison—who are above those in labor camps, who supersede the escapees to Sweden, Russia, and South

America. The key question being: Where did you spend the war? The more dire the circumstances, the more family murdered, the greater the starvation and disease, the higher the rung in this social register.

Most of my life I've been urged, goaded, and beseeched to remember. I even receive letters that begin "Dear Survivor" and end "We serve notice to the world that the Holocaust can never be forgotten, must never be repeated. Your commitment to bear witness must go on. We are not a people who forget."

Parrotlike, the Second Generation echoes the injunction of memory, the commandment Zachor. Remember. Remember what? Lives extinguished? Privates mutilated? Dead grandparents? Nonexistent uncles, aunts, cousins? Childhoods, entire countries and cultures lost? I knew no one. I had seen nothing. I had no personal experience of the war. Yet I was born on the other side, lived my first year in a refugee camp. My father had numbers, my mother nightmares, and I, their fierce, anxious love. I had almost not been born but for a whim, a white scarf, and an impulse to run into the forest.

"How can she write this about our family!" Genia cries out. "How dare she? Little stinker. *Pisher.* My Zosha! I gave her everything. And she does this? Humiliate all of us. In front of the Americans.

"It is our privacy! Zosha has watched us, taken notes, pinned Heniek and me to the page like butterflies, picking apart our wings to see the machinery."

Genia stands up, dropping all her daughter's carefully typed pages so they fall like white and black lies, fanning in a hundred directions.

"Let me tell you something, big shot. We're not the

ones who go to psychologists. The world was crazy, not us. After liberation, the Red Cross sent all kinds of doctors to inspect us. For typhus, tuberculosis, malaria, lice. You name it. Mental illness too. One day they sent this American doctor. I remember he looked very important, with a black beard, smoking a pipe.

"So he examined us. And you know what? He said he couldn't find a single crazy person except for one. 'There's a woman sitting in front of a piece of a glass,' he said, 'combing her hair with a broken comb.' Someone said to him, 'Did you offer her a good comb and a mirror?'"

Slowly, as if on her shoulders is a heavy package, Genia gathers the poison what her daughter writes, straightening the pages out carefully.

"It's true. I don't sleep well." She shakes her head back and forth. "I'm nervous. And yes, my Heniek is maniac, sometimes. Don't you think I know this? But this is nobody's business."

She stacks the pile of typed pages, laying them under the papers and manila folders. Making sure the drawer looks untouched, Genia kicks it shut with the heel of her shoe.

TRAUMA QUEEN

I wore black, of course. This was downtown, Seventeenth Street, corner of Second Avenue, an elementary public school where immigrants' children like yours truly, who spoke Yiddish or Polish at home, learned all the words to "Climb Every Mountain" and got a fierce case of the American dream. Abandoned, the building became a crack house for years until some artists cleaned it up, turning it into a gallery and performance space. A real New York story.

As I climbed two flights of dimly lit stairs, I checked out the walls, plastered with posters advertising an Eric Bogosian play, psychosexual dance, a poetry slam, living theater, and women's mime.

A small crowd milled outside a door with a poster of a yellow Star of David twisted around a swastika. Underneath it:

EXORCISMS
Rituals of Remembrance qnd Revenge
MARYSE EHRLICH

Maryse had approached me after hearing me read my poetry. Told me that she was 2G too, that her mother had killed herself, and handed me a flyer about her piece *Exorcisms*. At the time, I was less than curious. Now I stood in line at the box office. Checking out the competition.

"Have you read any reviews?" a woman with kinky blond hair whispered to her friend, a petite brunette in large red-framed glasses.

"Supposed to be *very* interesting," her friend answered. "Besides, I got TDF vouchers so it's half price."

When my turn came, I gave my name. The balding young man found it on a list and handed me a pair of comp tickets. I looked around to see if I could share my extra ticket. Oh shit! I groaned inwardly as I gazed across the lobby.

There stood Uly Oppenheim in his full, arrogant glory. Herr Holocaust Professor. Herr Fucker, talking to some woman in tight blue jeans. Hastily, I turned in the other direction.

We had not spoken since our one-night explosion. Afterward, he mentioned a wife who had converted and lit *Shabbos* candles. Of course, he'd be here.

Finally, the doors opened.

The crowd began to push forward. A pale man with bad skin, wearing a military coat and boots, stood at the door. He stopped each person, taking her ticket, then handed out a program and an envelope. He pointed silently inside.

White cushions lined the floor. Awkwardly, I dropped down, trying to find room for my legs. Inside the envelope, I discovered what looked like a nametag. There was a single hand-lettered word: AUSCHWITZ.

Holding it up, I turned to the woman sitting next to me. "Do you have one of these too?"

She showed me hers. RAVENSBRUK.

What's going on here?" I asked.

"I suppose we'll find out," she said, turning to look around herself.

She was attractive in a nose-job sort of way. White-skinned, petulant mouth. She was like Veronica in the comic strip. Snooty, imperious as hell. Was she 2G?

Instinctively, I looked around the room. My 2G Geiger counter rarely erred. That's what we called each other. The ones whose parents survived the war. I thought of 3G. My progeny, if I ever reproduced.

Sitting across the room, Uly noticed me. He raised his eyebrows. I nodded slightly. No thanks, I thought.

Mostly it was a downtown-artist-type crowd. They had paid twelve bucks a head and looked all fired up. Why? Around me, people flashed name tags that said DACHAU, TREBLINKA, BERGEN-BELSEN. Was it some kind of joke?

I turned my attention to the program. "Ms. Ehrlich was born in Lodz, Poland in 1947. Her mother and aunt went through the war together." I skimmed down the page. "Ehrlich was raised in Forest Hills, Queens . . . "

"Queens," I muttered. This time, the woman next to me, who I hoped might be an ally, did not respond.

A couple sat down on a cushion next to mine. The man, frizzy-haired, wore a Mickey Mouse T-shirt. He pinned his nametag in the center, over Mickey's nose. MAIDENEK. His date, a black woman with beaded dreadlocks, already wore hers: RADOM.

The lights dimmed. The man in military gear closed both doors with a loud bang. Probably Maryse's old man, I thought. Was he really German? A heavy chain clanged. The locks clicked. Several people turned around. Crossing his arms, the man positioned himself in front of the door.

Suddenly, slides flashed on the walls all around us. Photographs from concentration camps! The familiar, horrifying ones. A chiaroscuro of hollowed sockets, skeletal corpses dumped in cavities filled with mangled limbs, lineups at Nazi gunpoint.

Simultaneously, a tape began. The voices were in Polish, German, French. Then, English. A man cried: "Please don't hit me! Sir, please!" More cries, moans. A woman's voice wailing. "How can you do this? You are human, no?"

A thin spotlight framed Maryse Ehrlich as she commanded the center of the stage. Dressed in black, her body disappeared into the darkness. Her hair was pulled back severely from her face, lit like sculpture. The bold hawklike nose balanced an aggressive jaw. A grotesque mask, but I couldn't take my eyes off her face. So different from when I had met her. This was her show.

She took the microphone from a stand. "I dedicate this evening to my family, murdered in camps like these. The ones who never even survived in a photograph."

She looked around. "Fifty years ago, the Lodz ghetto was liquidated. Burned. Destroyed. Next month is the deathday." She paused. "I like to remember deathdays. Don't you think it's a fine idea? Like birthdays? And the great thing is you don't have to buy presents."

Controlling the remote, she flashed more images of

concentration camp victims. Emaciated, toothless faces staring out, bony limbs in striped pajamas. The wooden bunks. Showers. Death marches.

Some of the slides reflected on our cushions. There was a moment when I saw a dead skeleton at my feet.

Maryse's eyes circled the room like a falcon's. Then she commanded, "Bring up the lights, Hermann. I want to see our audience." There was absolute silence. We held our breath, not knowing what to expect.

The light from the projected atrocity slides made everyone's nametags glow. RAVENSBRUK, AUSCHWITZ, we flashed back and forth. Around us, TREBLINKA, BIRKE-NAU, DACHAU. The nametags of some nightmarish international convention. The woman next to me did not stir, her attention riveted.

"No response at all?" Maryse paused. "Look at the slides. Listen to the voices. For God's sake," she sneered, "this isn't TV. It really happened."

She stopped, took a deep breath. We sat there like expectant inmates. "Have you ever noticed how people will admit to almost anything? Except rage," she said. "'It's okay. Really. You can murder my family, my best friend. Castrate me.'"

She walked back a few feet. "We're all liars," she said. "We lie all the time about our anger."

Several people stood up. They walked to the door. "It's okay, Hermann," she motioned to the man in the back, "they can go. Is there anyone else who wants to leave? Come on. Get the fuck out if the heat's too strong."

The couple in front of us stood up. "I've had enough of this," the frizzy-haired man said. MAIDENEK glowed on his Mickey Mouse T-shirt.

"You want Chinese or Indian?" his date whispered.

I wanted to leave too. I didn't move.

The door slammed with shocking power. The lock clanged, then locked. We couldn't escape. Maryse began to stalk back and forth, gripping the microphone. "You know what? Your meekness makes me sick!" She spat out the words. "You just sit there and watch the slides. When are you going to stop being so pathetic? Don't you have any reaction at all?" Her eyes burned as she peered over us.

The audience stirred uncomfortably.

"They murdered, tortured, experimented on human beings. Shoved people into gas chambers. They thought they were going to take a shower. There were even cute soap dishes. Look at what those bastards did. Say it. You hate them," she hissed. "Say it, you weaklings! Hate!"

"Hate!" Someone called softly.

Her voice jeered. "Hate, *hate! Hate!*"

A few people began to chant "Hate! Hate!" Their voices grew louder.

"*Rage! Hate! Rage!* Don't you feel it? People stuck into ovens, their own brothers forced to push them in. Crematoria filling the air with the smell of flesh burning."

Several people seemed to cower from her as she screeched, "Hate, hate, hate! All of you are seething with it," she cried. "Don't be afraid of it. Hate! Hate! Hate!"

"Hate, hate, hate . . . " Voices chanted. A few people rose slowly to their feet. "Hate, hate, hate, hate . . . "

"Let out your repressed rage, you cowards. Scream it. Curse! What you feel about those murderers! The medical experiments. Don't be afraid. Collecting human hair, eyeglasses, dentures. Turn up the volume," she commanded. The taped voices grew terrifyingly loud. "DON'T KILL US. ISN'T IT ENOUGH YOU MURDERED MY FAMILY? PLEASE, SIR."

"Hate, hate, hate . . . " A few more people stood, their hands clenched in fists. Others followed.

"RAGE!" she shouted. "HATE!"

"Hate, hate! Bastards!" A cacophony of voices. I could see Uly beginning to chant softly. "Hate, hate, hate . . . "

"Rage, you assholes! Or are you too stupid and too scared, you castrates!"

People were shouting. "Motherfuckers! Die! I hate you!" Their faces lit by fervor. A long-haired girl in an Indian smock began to sob.

"Oh, shit," I said under my breath. "This is awful."

The woman next to me had joined the chant, her voice growing louder. "Hate, hate . . . " I felt like I was at a Hitler Youth rally.

Maryse's black eyes narrowed to lasers sweeping across the room, searching for an infidel, honing in, I could swear, on me. I quickly shifted my stare to the floor.

The voice of the woman next to me boomed as she chanted, "Hate, hate, hate . . . "

"Hate, hate, hate," Maryse roared into the microphone. "No one sits this one out. Don't you understand? There's no free ride."

Suddenly Maryse pointed to me. "You. You over there. Are you above this sort of thing?"

The voices screeched around me. "Hate, hate, hate!" People punched the air, pulling at their own hair as the tape wailed. "DON'T YOU SEE I AM DYING? JUST A *SHTICKEL* BREAD."

The microphone wire snaked behind her as she walked through the audience. "HATE, HATE, HATE, HATE, HATE!" she chanted, her voice hard and vicious, stepping past people huddled in groups on the floor. It wasn't my imagination. I would be her victim.

Desperately, I turned to the back of the room. The door was locked. The man stood guard against any interruptions.

"Don't look away from me," she ordered.

I met her preying eyes, her black uniform.

"Hate, hate, hate!" The people in the audience grew more agitated. "Kraut bastards, pigs!"

"Yes, you," she said, standing several feet from me. "Your father was in Auschwitz?" she asked, staring at my tag.

How did she know? Was it just a bizarre coincidence? I looked at Uly, who had stopped chanting. I nodded.

"And how much family did you lose?"

"Everyone," I whispered.

Maryse approached me. Standing over me, her face contorted with contempt. "Can't hear you."

"Everyone," I said louder.

"And your mother?" she demanded.

Someone nearby started to say something to her.

She turned on him. "I'm not talking to you!" She turned to the others. "Don't stop. HATE, HATE, HATE . . . "

"Czestochowa," I answered.

"Forced labor?"

I nodded.

"And I suppose you have lots of grandparents, cousins, uncles and aunts. A big happy family."

"No, I don't."

"So why are you sitting there like a docile lump? Don't you understand? They reduced your people to slaves, the ones they didn't shoot in the head, burn, gas—" She paused. "Like my family. And you're going to act like a good sport about it. Be a liberal? Broad-minded? Open your eyes to what's going on! HATE!" she brayed. "Say it, goddamn it!"

I said nothing.

"I can't hear you." She stood over me. "Don't you get it?" she rasped. "You're sitting on your power. Get up off the floor, you groveling mess!"

"HATE! HATE! HATE!" The word surrounded me like sludge as I rose to my feet. "HATE! HATE! HATE!"

I faced her squarely. "Go back to goddamn Queens!" I spat at her.

The door finally opened. I rushed out, found a toilet down one flight of stairs, went inside, and locked it. Facing the mirror, my tears heaved. Furious, self-pitying tears that turned my mascara into tiny black pebbles.

"Hate," I repeated the word bitterly, splashing water over my face.

Knocking. More knocking. "Just a moment!" I called, wiping my face with a paper towel.

I opened the door. Several women stood in line. I started for the stairs when I saw Uly. He approached me. "That was rough, kiddo." His voice was drenched with compassion.

"Do you call that theater?" I demanded.

"It was somewhat cathartic."

"More like sadistic," I said. "If I want therapy, I'll go back to my shrink."

"I think Maryse's onto something," he responded. "That's what I told her."

"You know her?" I asked.

"Not in the biblical sense." He smirked in his self-satisfied way, "But I'll probably interview her. Find out if she actually has a conceptual base to her work."

That's when it hit me. "You're going to fuck Maryse too," I said. "Aren't you?" I didn't wait for his answer.

IMAGINE AUSCHWITZ

I have this dream, except my eyes are open. There are tracks. Train tracks that transported people to death camps. They were old, young, sick, hungry, too insensible to trade a gold tooth for a breath. I walk on the tracks, overgrown with weeds.

Black wire fences with their arching posts stand on either side, and high above, the spindly legs of guard towers once mounted with rifles. This starkness, a landscape of ritual murder.

Yet it is lush. Verdant grass where once there was mud, body slime. Clusters of brilliant goldenrod. Wildflowers sprout everywhere. Bushes with tiny berries. Soil enriched by human mulch.

A young man in suede shorts and hiking boots approaches from the opposite direction. He is returning.

"Don't bother," he says, "There's nothing left to see at Birkenau." As he passes, his metal cup swings from his knapsack.

He's right, of course. Nothing to see, no education to be had from the open fields circumscribed by wires like a demonic grid. But I must go. The sun, brilliant all afternoon, begins its drop.

Looking ahead, I see a field covered with drops of blood. Millions of drops sparkling. Murdered Jewish blood. Walking closer, I discover a field of succulent red poppies, their petals plumped like mouths. The sun blazes as it drops into the horizon slit.

I come to the ramp of the train station. End of the line. Another Selection. That infamous pageant. Here. People were selected: right for murder, left for slave labor. I stare down the tracks. A transport could arrive. My mother's family. My father's.

I walk down the *Lagerstrasse*, the wide street that crossed from the women's camp to the men's. Past the quarantine camp and camp for families, Gypsy camp, the storage sheds of inmates' belongings called Canada. An abandoned ghost town of a death mall. The sun blazes above the tall poplars. Soon it will set. I stop at the broken brick and rubble, all that is left of the crematoria.

Why hadn't the Allies blown everything up after the war? Destroyed the evidence. The bestial victimization. Why save Hess's amusement park, complete with labeled hangman paraphernalia?

Behind the barracks, there's a small pool of murky water. Tall weeds and algae don't obscure its contents, a dump for human ash. The lagoon is empty, desolate as if its souls had fled. A crunching sound underfoot, amid grass fat with fertilizer. Bending over, I pick up a sliver of bone the size of a nail clipping.

Bones have a phosphorescent substance, I recall. They glow in the dark.

Running my hand over the ground, I discover more splinters of bones and, digging in further, the remains of a spoon.

Someone used it to eat a sorry portion of soup. I rub the charred surface, its twisted handle. Someone had carried it with her everywhere. As she burned, the spoon melted.

The sun's golden rays have grown gray, mauve clouds weaving a somber tapestry. Steam rises off the lagoon in whorls of smoke. Soon it will be dark.

What to do? Try to get back through the fields in the dark? Auschwitz with its hotel and two restaurants, bitter refuge, is several miles away. The poplars' shadows lengthen, their branches lurking.

I steal into the women's barracks, a long, narrow room with rows of bunks separated by brick partitions like cages in a chicken coop. Not enough room to sit. I lie down on one of the hard, narrow bunks that slept several women. The wood is damp. A bone-chilling draft.

What to do? Shivering, I grasp the thin cotton of my pullover. Should I try to run back? I look out the window frame. Darkness shrouds everything. Not even a moon and the sky, starless. *There isn't anything.* Head propped against the brick wall, I stare ahead.

I'm scared. The leaves hiss and a bitter wind blows through the bare windows. My teeth chatter as I lean against the cold brick wall of the barracks. Hours of darkness. The punishers lurk nearby. My eyes glow like bone splinters. I clutch my own body for warmth.

When I close my eyes, it is worse. The punishers attack like dogs, teeth flashing white, driven mad by the color red, saliva glistening.

The war isn't over. I am the *Musselman*, shuffling in a blue-and-white striped uniform, despising the model prisoners, my parents, for their mute helplessness. Orphans who had found each other at a refugee dance, clinging in terror and joy and finally as parents.

There is an injunction to live. No posthumous victories for Hitler. When one doesn't live, the devil triumphs. Had my parents survived so I, their only child, could put myself back into a concentration camp. Back? I'd never left.

I had spent years within its architecture. I was not supposed to leave, to have or want. Tattooed on my arm: *Must never forget, not even for a moment.* Because I lived when so many died.

Feeling my way in the darkness, I find the door. It is locked. Someone has locked me inside. It is 1944. The ghetto has been liquidated. I am to die. "Let me out!" I cry, banging my fist against the door. The wind blows it open. A death rattle of leaves against the barracks. Souls without bodies, hissing, murder without mercy.

In the daylight, these are just barracks. No one has slept in them for fifty years. Stepping outside, I see a field overgrown with weeds and sharp-toothed brush. An abandoned railroad track. These are historical artifacts. I start to run.

Past the barbed-wire grid. I leap over the rails, running on the tracks. The guard towers bleak as scarecrows. It is no longer nightmare country. Just a rural landscape. A gray morning. Tourist buses are already arriving at Auschwitz.

I find a uniformed guard. "Excuse me. Where's a telephone?"

"Cafeteria," he says with a Polish accent. "Right off the parking lot."

I walk through a large modern room with white Formica tables and a long counter on which sandwiches, bowls of salad, plastic-wrapped pastries, and French rolls are displayed. I think of the turbid soup, the crusts of bread they had eaten to survive. Why not show that? There are tiny bottles of *vin rouge*. The smell of strong coffee wafts in my nostrils. Though my stomach groans with hunger, I know I can't touch this food.

"Mom—"

"Where are you?"

"Is Daddy all right?"

"Yes, everyone is fine. Where are you?"

"Auschwitz."

"They have phones there? Heniek!" she calls. "Pick up the phone. Heniek, it's Zosha. Pick up!" she screams. "He must be on the toilet," she mutters. "Have you been eating?"

I hear a click, a line opens.

"Where are you?" my father demands.

"Auschwitz."

"They have phones there, Heniek."

Silence.

"Talk to your daughter. It's collect long-distance."

"So how do you like it?" he asks.

"There are a lot of tourists."

"What do you think?" he asks. "Did you learn anything?"

"Daddy," I begin to weep. "I—"

"Oh, no, she's crying," he says.

"You always make her cry," my mother scolds.

I stand in front of the famous iron archway, facing the black letters. ARBEIT MACHT FREI. *Work Makes You Free*. Sure. You could die of starvation and exhaustion, and escape through the chimney.

It looks like a theater marquee. The entrance to a children's sleep-away camp. Picking up a large stone, I hurl it. The iron clangs. ARBEIT MACHT FREI.

RESURRECTION

Fragrant, about to find pups, apron-up, bagged, broken-knee'd, clucky, cocked-up, double-ribbed, enciente, full of heir, gone to seed, gravid, having a dumpling on, a hump in front, nine-months dropsy, one's cargo aboard, high-bellied, how-came-you-so, in a fix, dutch, pod, in the pudding club, Irish toothache, jumbled-up, ketched, kidded, knapped, knocked-up . . .

I had been pregnant once before. The father was Ludwig, whom I had perhaps loved more than anyone else. "I can control myself," he promised as he pulled out of me eighteen years ago. Coitus interruptus. What did I know?

"Are you positive?" I had asked Dr. Klotchkoff in naïve wonder.

For several days, I let the miracle wash over me. I walked the streets of Manhattan in a maternal haze, filled with the thick, fecund sensation of being female, carrying a new life. I imagined a beautiful boy with a rosebud penis, Ludwig's straight brown hair, and my mother's green eyes. A girl with his lustrous doe eyes; my dark, unruly hair; my father's cleft chin.

It would have been a baby of love, begotten of youthful passion. I had imagined that Lud and I, son of a German and daughter of Jewish Holocaust survivors, could heal a terrible world. Swords to ploughshares, Ludwig said. *Tikkun olam.*

It was impossible, of course. I was nineteen, in my second year of college. The illegal abortion was performed by a Queens obstetrician while his waiting room filled with mothers and wailing babies. He gave me a shot of morphine for the pain and threatened to stop if I continued to scream. The procedure cost eight hundred dollars, which I paid for with my savings. Ludwig had no money. We broke up soon afterward.

Sometimes I thought of Ludwig. Wondered what his life turned out to be. I thought of the child too. Adolescent now. A boy? A girl? A high school senior. And I would have been a mother, as I had assumed over the years I would never be.

Yet I had been raised to have babies. To give them names of murdered family members. Perele, Rutka, after my father's sisters. Zalmen, his father. Jesse, my mother's beloved brother. I couldn't possibly have enough children to carry the names of all the dead. So I had none.

How could it have been so easy?

My mother had aborted twice in Germany before I was born, and a third time afterward, though recently she had mentioned a fourth. "You know, every time your Dad looked at me, I got pregnant," she explained.

So it was a tradition, if you could call two females in a family line a tradition. This careless disregard for human life. A paradox, really. As if the dead martyrs, who were revered, were more important than the living. My mother, so pretty, opening her Vivien Leigh eyes wide so that all could see her beauty. As if life were so very casual, when she had survived by a hangnail.

For me, death was a pure abstraction. There had been no one left to die. I had never even been to a funeral.

The first time I met Avi was in his yellow cab. He had picked me up with my rolling suitcase at La Guardia Airport. I had just returned from several months of living at the Chateau Marmont in Hollywood, where I was working on a script about a girl's street gang in the early 1960s for Universal Studios.

Once, I had been Dr. Shlock, concocting *bubbe meises* about movie stars, fanciful fictions about Liz and Dick, Cher, Jackie, and Elvis's last words from the grave. Still a freelancer, I was now more gainfully employed by several studios as a script doctor. They sent me screenplays in overnight pouches, often as awesome in their awfulness as was the money involved in pre-production. My job was to try to create characters from stereotyped notions of human nature molded entirely from decades of sitcom-watching by mostly young, mostly male writers. I was so glad to be back in New York I could have kissed the cabbie.

"Avi Ben-Tzion." I read his license aloud as we drove along the Long Island Expressway. "Israeli?"

He nodded without turning around.

"How long have you lived in New York?"

"Many years," he answered in his lightly accented English. "I'll take the Queensboro, okay? There shouldn't be any traffic."

"I visited Israel in nineteen sixty-seven," I remarked. "Right after the war."

"That was a high time for us."

"What about now?"

"Israelis are too busy spending money, buying electronic junk. Imitating you Americans."

I let it pass, rejoicing to myself: I hadn't come across a rude Israeli cab driver in some time. "Have you been driving for a long time?"

He shrugged. "Look, I'm an artist. I do my work. I have my shows. Occasionally, when I need money for paint and canvas, I drive for a few days."

"Were you born in Israel?"

"Europe," he answered impatiently. "Poland, if you want to know."

I didn't say anything.

"*Right* after the war," he added. "Nineteen forty-six."

"Your parents were in the camps," I said.

He nodded.

"Mine too," I responded. "But I was born in Germany."

"Shoah." Avi pronounced the single word as if it explained everything.

"Your parents went directly to Israel?"

"What are you doing? Interviewing me?" he asked.

For the rest of the ride, neither of us spoke. It seemed we'd exhausted our capacity for conversation, or at least I had exhausted his. But when we got to my street, he turned around and gave me something. "Here."

"I don't need a receipt."

"Why don't you look at it?"

I was surprised to discover a business card. *Studio Bentzion* was printed in a jagged type with his name and phone number.

Avi Ben-Tzion. I had a chance to look at him for the first time. Thick brown hair streaked with gray, fair complexion, a good, strong face. A paper-cut scar arced the skin under his left eye, continuing in a diagonal across his cheek.

"I thought I had really turned you off," I said. "My American talking."

"You're not an American."

"I came here when I was one and a half."

"It doesn't matter. Come and see my work if you like," he said. "Then we can talk."

Several nights later, we met at China de Cuba in Chelsea.

A wave of Chinese immigrants had arrived in Cuba during the 1920s. Their offspring invented this perfect combination for the restless New York palate: *ropa vieja* (old clothes) with egg rolls, shrimp lo mein, yellow rice and black beans, and wonton soup. Salsa and soy. Fortune cookies too.

He chose a red booth by the window. I shimmied in next to him. The Cuban-Chinese decor was as schizo as the food. Bright fluorescent lights with red paper lanterns, Chinese calendars, red paper mats, gold lettering, enormous, unnegotiable red menus with Cuban dishes listed first, in Spanish and English, followed by Chinese dishes.

"I can't deal with this menu," he said, putting it aside.

"I don't mind ordering for us," I suggested.

"Good." He seemed to relax.

A plate of steamed dumplings arrived, followed by

fried plantains. "I hope you don't mind," I said, dipping a dumpling into the hot sauce. "I've been wanting to ask you something."

He looked at me curiously.

"How did you get—this?" I pointed to the scar.

"You want to know? Nothing big. A car accident. The windshield exploded in my face." He looked at me. "Does it repel you?"

I reached out to touch his scar, my finger tracing its path on his face, under his eye. "It feels so smooth."

We drove to Fort Greene, Brooklyn, where Avi had a studio on a scary, empty block in an abandoned glass factory. He operated the industrial elevator by turning a key. The iron doors clanged open on the sixth floor.

He turned on a board of switches. Suddenly, thousands of electrical watts flooded the room. And everywhere, there were canvases on white walls.

I moved around the room slowly, still partly blinded by the light. The living area was separated from the studio by a rice-paper screen. Once my eyes grew accustomed, I saw black-outlined figures painted on vividly colored canvases. Strong, familiar, but unexpected images. Then I recognized these were biblical characters, taken out of the desert of thousands of years ago and placed in modern Israel. Jacob wrestling with the angel on Ben Yehuda Square in Jerusalem as couples sit and flirt at Café Atar. Sarah and Hagar portrayed as two haggling women, pulling each other's hair in the Mehane Yehuda market. King David as a young man, streaking across Dizengoff in Tel-Aviv, amid sexy billboards.

Polaroids were taped next to the paintings on the walls as well as slips of paper with sketches and handwritten jottings. There were stacks of books in Hebrew and English.

"You're good!" I declared, relieved that I could be honest.

"Good enough to drive a taxi." His voice sounded rueful.

"And get me to come to Brooklyn to see what you do when you're not driving a taxi," I said. "What are these?"

There were several eight-foot oil canvases with a single naked, gaunt specter suspended in the center in a kind of agonized limbo.

"These are ancestors too," he said. "I recognize them."

"I don't show these, though."

"Why?"

"I was raised in a country of Jews, of survivors who had emigrated after the war. Formed in the image of strength—*gevura*—and self-discipline. Don't look back. Everyone a soldier. One day a year, Yom Hashoah, we remembered the Holocaust."

"That was it?"

"That was it. Otherwise, we didn't indulge in psychology and we made fun of America's Shoah business with all its wealthy survivors."

"You know, there were no such thing as survivors when I was growing up," I told him. "I heard the word *refugees* or *victims*. *Martyrs*, even. Never *survivors*."

"Everyone's a survivor nowadays," he remarked. "My parents rarely mentioned the war. But whenever a *yortzeit* came up, and they had many, they lit candles, getting this other-world look in their eyes. But if you asked them about it, they just shook their heads."

Then he looked intently at me. "And then there were the real things that were happening around us. Bus stations and cafes blowing up in your face, stores on Dizengoff, our Broadway, exploding with glass and fire," he said, shaking his head. "That's how I got this." He pointed to the scar. "When a bomb blew up in the Jerusalem bus station."

"Why did you lie to me?"

"I don't like to get into it."

I ran my finger gently over the scar.

I watched, that first night, as he stripped down to purple bikini briefs. Avi was muscular, built close to the ground, long waist, narrow hips, thick chest hair with silver curls. Before he turned the lights off, he lit a candle. A white Sabbath candle.

"Is it Shabbos?" I asked.

"For me it is," he answered.

"And for me," I agreed. "You should only know." It had been longer than I cared to remember since I'd been intimate with a man.

Avi pulled off my sweater, unhooked my bra, his fingers exploring. I lay down next to him. His eyes were closed. I kissed his face, gently touching his scar with my lips. It was taut as a guitar string.

Oh! I cried out in pleasure as Avi moved over my body with his fingertips. How he outlined me, brushstrokes filling in large areas, then fine-tuning with his lips over the canvas of my skin. I reached out for him.

Over the next few months, we spent most of his nights off together. There was fire in our bed and great affection, but we never mentioned the future. What I knew was that he had been married for a short time, had a son, Yonah, who was now grown. He had been living alone in New York for seven years.

"Why did you leave?" I asked one evening after we had

polished off several cartons of Chinese food at his loft. Now we drank beer, Chinese, of course, from a wine-sized bottle.

"That's very sensitive for most Israelis," he said. "There's a Hebrew word. *Yordim.* It means 'gone down,' one who has left Eretz Yisrael."

"Talk about guilt manipulation."

"If you want to know, it's because I had to," he went on tensely. "After the accident, I got a bad case of nerves. I couldn't ride the bus anymore. I kept thinking I saw bombs in paper bags. It was just someone's lunch. I was too anxious to drive. I thought I was leaving for a short time, but I never went back."

I reached over, starting to rub his shoulders.

"Oh, that feels sweet." He poured more beer into our glasses.

Why is this night different from all other nights?

I stood transfixed before the bathroom mirror several weeks later. *What if?* What if I didn't put it in? The door to possibility sprang open before my eyes. I could have a child. A Jewish child. I would be a mother. *Me!* I opened the blue plastic case and stared at the rubber disc in the plastic case, in the shape of a *yarmulke.*

A reverie of names spun in my head. A baby girl called Pearl. Zalmen, if he was a boy, except I'd change it to Sam. Or maybe Jesse.

"Did you drown in there?" Avi called.

"I'll be right out." I snapped the blue plastic case shut.

He lay naked, waiting for me. I got into bed, next to him. Avi placed a green satin pillow under my hips. "Are you ready?"

"Make me ready."

That night, millions of spermatozoa, whipping their long tails, spiraled upstream to find a solitary waiting ovum. While Avi and I slept in each other's arms, a microscopic cell, inscribed with our genetic cuneiform, began its exponential split.

Several weeks later, when nausea overcame me. I plunked down fourteen dollars for a plastic cup and dipstick. What a rip. Later, I slowly submerged the white stick into my humble cup of piss.

Nothing happened.

Then, suddenly, a slow reddening like a blush. I held my breath. *The dawn of man!* It spread across the plastic tip, turning the nib a bright baby pink.

I held it up like a thermometer, then reread the instructions on the package. "These tests are not 100% reliable." It had happened. I was with child.

I thought of my cousin Lusia, who had married Greg, a gentle Catholic man, and was childless. She said that she thought the universe was too evil a place to bring children into. She knew, having watched her mother starve to death in Auschwitz. "We love our dogs," she said fondly. "They are our babies."

Maryse Ehrlich, fellow 2G and performance artist, confided, "I know my limitations, Zoe. I'm too narcissistic to have children. I'm just too depressive. I won't even have a dog. Besides, I like to travel."

"How can I be anybody's mother?" I implored Christine, my good friend from our movie fanzine days.

"Why not?" she asked me over coffee at one of the last remaining Broadway diners, where I. B. Singer used to drink tea and write his stories.

"It's not me." I shook my head vehemently. "I wish it were, but it's not. I don't have those kinds of instincts."

"Zoe, wait a minute," she urged. "You didn't use anything, right?"

I nodded sheepishly. "What an idiot I am."

"Why didn't you?"

"I didn't want to. At that moment I wanted a baby. I must have been crazy."

"Maybe you weren't crazy. Maybe you were perfectly, calculatedly sane, making a decision for your future. You could surrender, Zoe," she said. "Join the human race."

I paced nervously as Avi walked into my apartment that evening."I got some *ganja* from this Jamaican at work," he said. "Do you want to light up?"

I shook my head.

"That's not like you, Zoe."

"I'm not in the mood."

"What's up?"

I handed him the pink-tipped plastic dipstick.

"A Popsicle stick?" He turned it around in his delicate fingers.

"A pregnancy test," I said.

His eyes grew large. "You aren't?"

I nodded.

His face registered shock. "Weren't you using your—?"

"I don't remember," I answered, avoiding his eyes.

"It matters to me," he said. When I didn't answer, he finally asked softly, "Why?"

"I want to have a baby, I guess."

"But we didn't even talk about it."

"You're right."

He shook his head. "I didn't need this, Zoe. It's what

happened with Chen. She got pregnant, we got married, then we had a real mess."

"I'm sorry," I said.

"I need some air," he said, standing up.

"I'll come with you."

"Not now," he said, closing the door behind him.

Lady in waiting, lap-clap, loaded, looking piggy, lumpy, lusty, pillowed, pizened, poddy, poisoned, preggy, pumped, sewed-up, short-skirted, shot in the giblets, in the tail, storked, stung by a serpent, swallowed a watermelon seed . . .

Avi didn't return. It was a hard night. As I tried to sleep, voices of the ghosts cried out. *Name me. Give me your child. Resurrect our lost lives. Breathe life into your life, Zosha.*

Sunday morning. I woke up slowly, then, startled, I remembered! I rubbed my belly like a chimpanzee. A house was being built here for new life. I could feel it. As I stepped out of the shower, the doorbell rang.

Avi stood in my doorway, holding a brown bag of warm H & H bagels like an offering.

"I know I should've called," he said. "I went back to my studio last night and stared at the walls." He reached out for me. I held back.

"What can I say?" He shifted his weight. "I needed some time."

"Come in."

For several moments, we looked at each other uncomfortably. Finally, I broke the silence. "Avi, I've decided that I'm going to have this baby."

"Oh?"

Then added quickly. "By myself."

"Not so fast," he said.

"Avi, you don't have to go through this again. "

"Who knows? Maybe it's *bashert*." He took my hand in his. "Do you know what that is?'

"Meant to be?"

He nodded. Then Avi lowered himself slowly, crouching, his head against my belly. *"Shema Yisrael adonoi elohaynu,"* he began to recite. *"Adonoi ehad."*

I recoiled in disgust, pushing him away.

"What's the matter?"

"Why'd you do *that*?"

"Do you know what the Shema is?" he asked, standing up.

"That's what people said when they were dying in the gas chambers."

"It's more than that, Zosha. 'Listen, God is all,'" he translated, "'and all is one.'" He stared at me. "Yes, it's the last thing we say before we die." He paused. "But it will be our child's first prayer."

That's when I lost it, tears stinging my eyes.

"I'll probably have to drive more hours," Avi said practically.

Several weeks later, it was Passover. I brought Avi home.

"Come, sit," my mother urged us, pulling his arm. Avi and I sat down on the couch, white crushed velvet with olive green tentacles. It had been covered in clear plastic for a decade, until my mother's cousin, Helah, came to visit in the summer. Her buttocks got stuck and made an awful sound when she tried to stand up. And so the couch was finally exposed.

My mother had cleaned several hundred slivers of glass in the chandelier, polishing them until they shone like mirrors. The table was covered with a white damask tablecloth, a ceremonial holiday plate in the center, haggadahs from Maxwell House and Manischewitz at the side of each plate.

Batya, my mother's distant cousin, who went to Cuba after the war, was invited with Anya, a fifty-year-old nurse's aide from Warsaw. "In our home, my mother set such a beautiful table," Batya recalled as she sat down at the table. "We were twenty, twenty-two people at our seder." Then looking around herself, she asked, "Is Esther coming?"

"Who's Esther?" my father demanded.

"Her sister," my mother whispered.

"Where's Esther?" Batya repeated.

My father growled in frustration. "She's not here," he said loudly. "She died."

Avi grinned at me. He enjoyed my parents because they reminded him of his own.

Batya eyed me suspiciously. "You're not Esther."

"Of course not," Anya told her. "That's Zosha. Genia's daughter."

"Who's Genia?" she asked.

"*Veys mir*," my father groaned. "Let's get started. Genia!" he shouted. "Where's the wine?"

My father raised an engraved silver goblet from his parents' home in Lodz. After the war, he had found it with a pair of carved silver candlesticks, which his father had buried behind their apartment building. The goblet glittered in the chandelier lights as he began reciting the Hebrew prayer for the fruit of the vine, as his father had done before the war. "*Baruch atah . . .* "

At thirty-nine, I was still the youngest in the group. So I had to read the four questions in Hebrew. "Why is this night different from all other nights?"

After I finished, my mother rose immediately. "Come, Zosha. The gefilte fish."

"One minute, please." Avi stood up, turning to my father. "I'd like to ask a fifth question." He paused.

"*Nu*," my father said impatiently.

"May I have your daughter's hand in marriage?"

My parents, rarely surprised, never speechless, suddenly were both.

My mother placed my hand hastily in Avi's as if she were afraid he might change his mind.

"There is other news too," Avi said. I watched their expressions.

"What kind of news?" My father sounded suspicious.

"Good news," I added.

"Mr. Palovsky," Avi said. "You're going to be a grandfather. And you, Mrs. Palovsky—" He turned to my mother. "You will be a grandmother. We're expecting a child." Avi beamed.

"*Boje, boje*," Heniek exclaimed in Polish. God, God.

"So much news," Genia murmured to herself. "So little news for so many years." She shook her head. "Too much news at one time."

"Are you happy?" I asked her.

"Oh, yes!" she cried. "You know, at my temple, people were always asking me. Why aren't you married? Such a good-looking girl. I prayed every Shabbos. And it worked!"

I had my amnio on a Wednesday. The TV monitor showed a nearly transparent filament swimming, its heartbeats exploding in tiny stars. Sunday was our wedding day.

Sunshine flooded Central Park on a May afternoon after a week of rain, and New Yorkers seemed happy to be alive.

Avi wore a black tuxedo, purchased from my cousin in the business. My dress was an off-white silk chemise with an overlay of lace covering my waist, which had expanded considerably.

An out-of-work actor, Jason, picked us up in a freshly painted blue rowboat. He popped open a bottle of champagne, then rowed us across the lake to the Boathouse, where our guests waited.

The Boathouse in Central Park was a secret artists and lunatics hangout. You could spend hours with a notebook and a cup of hot chocolate, the sun beaming on your face. That's how a famous poet with leonine gray hair always had a Florida tan. A real restaurant was about to open and expel us, so it seemed like the perfect place to cater our wedding.

My father gave me his arm, and I walked down the aisle supported by him. He looked puffed up with pleasure, peacock-proud in his navy brocade jacket and white ruffled shirt, courtesy of the same cousin. My mother stood nearby, movie-star beautiful, draped in aquamarine silk matched to the color of her eyes, sparkling with tears.

Christine clutched one aluminum post of the canopy, weeping into a blue handkerchief. Next to her, two of Avi's painter friends grasped the other ends. Maryse held hers, staring in wonder. Who had ever thought I would stand under a *chuppah* with a loving husband and a full heart and womb?

"We crush this glass, actually a light bulb—they're easier to break," said Rabbi Neal Finkle, a young Reconstructionist, who wore a tie-dyed *tallit*. "To symbolize the destruction of the Temple, the ways in which our world is broken."

The rabbi turned to Avi. "You, Avi Ben-Tzion . . . " Then he looked at me. "And you, Zosha Palovsky, are breaking with the past because you've come together to start something new, to begin a family. To mend our world, nearly destroyed by hatred . . . "

The rabbi wrapped the light bulb in a white napkin and placed it on the floor. He gave a signal by lifting his eyebrows. I held my breath. Avi raised his left foot and crushed the glass.

BLUE PARADISE

The setting sun casts shadows on the white walls of a small bungalow in Blue Paradise. An old man sits with a dark-haired boy at the kitchen table. He wears a beige cardigan sweater, a plaid woolen scarf around his throat. It is a cool evening in July.

He opens a brown manila envelope. Hundreds of stamps spill out.

"Wow!" the eight-year-old cries out. "Where'd you get all these?"

"I used to collect when I was your age," my father says. "Look at this one from Germany." He points to a blue stamp with a red locomotive.

"Are these from when you were a kid?"

He shakes his head. "We lost everything during the war. These I got in America."

"Deutsch-land Bundes-post," his grandson sounds out the words. "Have you been to Germany?"

"Of course. We lived there after the war. Your mother was born in Germany."

"Are you a German?" he asks, looking at me curiously.

"No, Jesse," I break in. "I came here when I was a baby. Then I became an American citizen. Remember, I told you all about that."

"Am I an American citizen?" he asks.

"Through and through," I answer.

"You're a first-generation American citizen," my father declares, then asks, "Where was I born?"

"Auschwitz?" he asks unsurely.

"Jesse!" I say. God, I hope my father doesn't start yelling at him.

"No. Auschwitz was a concentration camp," he answers patiently. "I was there during the war, but we're from Lodz, Poland. You must know these things."

"He knows, Dad."

That we were despised, that we were murdered. Jesse knows the magic number too. Six million. How could he not? But he also knows his grandparents, as I never knew mine.

"I'll remember, Papa." He beams at his grandfather. "I promise."

"Jesse, you know what you are?" He ruffles his hair. "A *mensch*."

I never knew this man, who takes such pleasure in a child. Maybe that's the gift of age. The gift of being able to grow old, as no other member of his family could, old enough to love a grandchild.

"Papa, I don't want to look at stamps anymore," says Jesse, standing up. "Is that all right?"

"Sure." My father stands up too and totters shakily over to the TV set. He turns on CNN and sits down in his La-Z Boy. My father, who slaved his whole life, swings back, his slippered feet flying in the air like blackbirds.

"Ah," he sighs. "It's good."

I've returned to the summers of my childhood, to Blue Paradise in the Catskills, where my parents own one of a dozen white bungalows with green trim arranged in a square. You can still see the letters B UE PAR D SE painted on a whitewashed handball court where no one has played since the children grew up.

Blue Paradise is a *shtetl*, where Polish and Yiddish are spoken, except when there's an American around like me. Then the people parade their formal, strongly accented, strenuously articulate English.

"So you're a writer," Tusha Rosenberg, a widow with a vividly dyed black hairdo, confronts me. "Tell me something. Why do you writers have to write so much about sex? Sometimes I feel that I have to take a shower after I read."

Their days are charmed. They bake the crumb cakes and almond crescent cookies of their childhood, sharing recipe secrets with each other. C*holent,* a heavy beef, onion, bean, and potato stew simmers for over twenty-four hours on my mother's stove in the middle of the summer. They make *galler*, that most disgusting of Eastern European delicacies—boiled beef hooves, which turn into a white jelly. Blue Paradise is heaven on earth.

When I was little, a chorus of Lola, Stella, Minka, Ruzha, Fela, Blanca, Lusia, Manusha, who all knew each other in Germany after the war, sat outside our bungalow, playing cards. Shrieking with laughter, they tweezed each other's brows and gave each other Toni permanents, wrapping pieces of hair in toilet paper. Ruzha gossiped while Manusha and my mother sat with their faces covered in Crisco shortening.

The husbands traveled on Route 17, arriving on Friday evenings, smelling of hard work and the humid city, bodies aching to submerge in the swimming pool. My father drove up on Saturdays, having worked the night shift. He tied the white string of his ancient maroon trunks. Easing his tired, pale body into the water with a loud, mournful sigh, he disappeared. Now the swimming pool is empty. "*Zimny,*" my father shivers. Cold.

Later, when we are about to start eating, my father screams at my mother. "Genia, you don't know what you're doing. That's wrong! Let me!" He grabs the electric knife from her hands, clasped as in prayer, over the roast beef.

My mother is about to shout at him. She would have in earlier years, but now her expression turns tender. "Heniek, don't exert yourself," she chides him. "And please, be careful with the knife."

It is the evening of our relationships. These tough, ghetto-fighting camp survivors are moving slowly toward the end of their lives. The family drama, or the family opera, in our case, has diminished to a poem, to a prayer, to the day when we will say Kaddish.

Afterward, I find my mother in the kitchen, her fiefdom since biblical times. "That was a good roast, no? Moist," she says. "Soft like butter. Here."

This is my mother, I muse, as I sponge the counter. She has lived through my exploits, public and private. She's known them intuitively. And I have lived through her to reach back to ancestral soil.

I remember the time she was called to my school, P. S. 28. I stood like a hostage in the principal's office.

"Your daughter was caught cheating on a math test," said Mrs. Washington, my fifth-grade teacher.

"No, I wasn't."

She raised the sleeve of my blouse to reveal numbers, drawn with blue ink on my forearm. "Look."

My mother's eyes met mine. I could see her shock.

"Thank you for telling me," Genia said stiffly. "I'll take care of it."

When we were outside, she screamed, "You're not normal!"

Spitting on her handkerchief, she tried to rub out the numbers. The blue ink resisted. She continued, spitting and rubbing, wiping the tears that flowed from her eyes on her sleeve. Slowly, the numbers began to unwrite themselves.

"How could you do such a disgusting thing?" she cried.

"I wanted to be like you!" I answered.

Just as I marched in her high heels, donned her black pillbox hat with the veil, imitated how she opened her mouth when she applied her red lipstick.

"What are you talking about?" she demanded.

"Will I have a tattoo when I get older?" I asked.

At that moment, my mother unbuttoned the sleeve of her shirtwaist dress. "Look, idiot! Your father has numbers, not me."

Genia turns off the water faucet. "So did you bring something nice to wear for tonight?" my mother asks me.

"What's tonight?"

"*Nu.* It's Saturday night. There's entertainment at the casino."

"Oh."

Always, it's been a casino, not a social hall. Casino, with all that Las Vegas razzle-dazzle. Actually, it's a wood-paneled room that resembles a finished basement except it's above ground.

"Arnie Keller," my mother continues. "An excellent zinger. He sang with Eddie Fisher. There's bagels and lox from the Fish Man. I paid for you already so you can take it home if you like. And what about Jesse?" she asks. "Does he have something?"

"I didn't even think of it."

She shakes her head. "What a person wears is important. Put on something decent, please."

Then she disappears in a ritual I remember from childhood. When she returns, she will look different, as if a fairy godmother came to her bedroom and turned her *shmattes* into golden finery. Several minutes later, she appears in a blue jumpsuit ensemble she's sewn from a Vogue pattern. Her hair is poufed and sprayed, her earrings, faux-sapphire, match the blue of the jumpsuit as does her sparkling eye shadow. She wears pantyhose and black patent leather heels.

We walk the several yards to the casino. Chagall reproductions taped to the walls, photographs of Barbra Streisand in *Yentl*, Jackie Mason, Ben Gurion, and Golda Meir, *Schindler's List* and Holocaust remembrance posters.

During the week, they play rummy-Q, pinochle, and poker, but tonight, an elderly man in a reddish toupee and flashy green jacket sits at an electric keyboard. He's singing, "Raindrops keep falling on my head" as we enter the casino.

Immediately, people rush up to us. "Oh, Zosha!" cries Mala, who shaves her eyebrows, penciling new moons. "You haven't changed one bit!"

"Such a beauty!" says Stella, touching my face. "Do you color your hair?" She used to work at the cosmetic counter at Stern's.

They still treat me like a miracle. My son is a normal miracle, an American miracle, like their own prosperity. But I was their Landsberg miracle, a child born in Europe after the war, before the survivors were relocated.

"And what about your husband?" asks Minka.

"Avi's working in the city," I answer, just as my mother had all those years.

Yes, I married, a fellow 2G—with a different pedigree, though. His parents emigrated to Israel after the war.

"And is that the young man?" Pola asks, smiling seductively. She is the first and only divorcée in their group. Jesse knows enough to lean back to avoid cheek-pinching. "Will you sing for us again?"

He grins at her. "Maybe."

"Come, Jesse," says his grandfather. "Have a bagel."

"I don't want a bagel," he answers.

"You hardly ate anything at supper. Come," he insists.

"Such a bad eater," my mother tsks.

Jesse rolls his eyes at me as he follows behind my father.

My mother takes me by the hand to visit her friends sitting at card tables around the dance floor. This is a proud, well-dressed group, like a giant cousin club whose members moved far away after the war, to Australia, South Africa, Israel. Now they spend their summers together again.

"You remember, Moshe," my mother says politely.

"Ach, Zosha!" His eyes are bloodshot, this lascivious flirt who has been pawing me since I was a teenager. He's grown heavy, his face red and meaty. "You look good enough to—" he says, smirking.

"How's Marlene?" I ask about his daughter, whom I used to know.

"Don't ask." He shakes his head. "This is a miserable life."

My mother nudges me to keep walking. "She lives with another woman. You know," she whispers. "Poor man."

Each year, one member doesn't make it back to the colony. Another unveiling in a distant Long Island cemetery follows. More bungalows stand empty in Blue Paradise. A white candle burns in a darkening glass.

We approach Edek and Bronia, who live near my mother in Florida. Bronia, whose son is an anesthesiologist, asks me, "You heard of Art Spiegelman?"

"Of course, *Maus* won the Pulitzer."

"A comic book about the Holocaust. In bad taste," my mother says. "But what do I know? I'm not a writer like you are."

"Mice and cats," my father's voice rises. "It was nothing. A piece of garbage."

I look over at Jesse. He is talking to the musician, who is letting him play random notes on his keyboard.

"I knew Wolf Blitzer's parents," says Shoshana, whose boyfriend is a professor of literature at Queens College. "You know, the one on the news on CNN. They lived near us in Washington Heights."

"Zosha, it's a good thing you come to visit your Mommy. Our children have grown up, left home. They rarely visit."

"Do you remember Henry Kissinger's parents?" asks Miecho. "They had an apartment on Fort Washington Avenue."

"What's it all about, Alfie ..." croons Arnie Keller. Several couples rise, the men taking their partners' arms, floating to the dance floor. Arthur Murray doesn't have

anything over these couples who really know their moves, twirling in unison.

"Did you have a bagel?" my father asks me.

I shake my head. "Not yet."

"Eat something. Do you want a drink?"

"I'll get it," I say. "Mom, a screwdriver?"

"I don't know," she says unsurely. "It always goes to my feet."

This must be a Polish expression because most people talk about liquor going to their heads. But for my mother, it is always her feet. She sits down at a table with my father.

The musician sounds the first notes of the "Theme from Dr. Zhivago."

"You know how to dance?" my father asks me.

He takes me out on the smooth wood floor, placing his arm firmly around my waist. "One-two-two-one, one-two-two-one," he counts softly, pressing the small of my back. He is wearing a freshly starched, short-sleeved cotton shirt. I brush my hand past the blue numbers on his arm. My mother smiles as she watches her husband of over fifty years dance with her no longer young daughter.

"Did you see that film on Channel Thirteen, *In Our Own Hands*?" asks Viktor, a tall man with a single dark eyebrow strung across his forehead.

"The one about the Jewish Brigade?" says Zamul, who emigrated to Israel after the war. "Sure. I lived that movie."

"We're not the ones that need to see that movie," my father says. "The Americans do."

"No matter what we talk about," remarks Abe, a furrier who made my mother's mink coat, "we always end up back at the Holocaust."

"Soon there will be none of us left." Viktor shrugs. "Who will remember?"

My father looks doubtfully at me. "Ach, maybe it's better they don't remember too much."

Pola approaches our table. "Please, Genia. Ask your grandson to sing. He has such a nice voice." Last year, he had wowed them with his voice so pure and high, singing "Take Me Out to the Ballgame."

"Do you want to sing?" she asks Jesse.

"You don't have to if you don't want to," I add.

"Sing for us, *kindeleh*," says the musician. "What do you know? *Hava Nagila*?"

"I want to sing my own song," Jesse says.

"He wants to sing his own song," the musician repeats. "Okay, ladies and gentlemen," he announces over the microphone. "We have a special guest. What's your name, kid?"

Jesse looks down from the raised stage. I hold my breath. Then he digs into his pocket and pulls out a hat and a pair of dark glasses. Slipping them on, he cracks a huge grin as he begins his Will Smith rap.

> *We are the Men in Black*
> *the only chosen members*
> *the good guys are dressed in black*

Men in Black? Chosen members? I have a vision of Jesse with a group of Hasids in Williamsburg, dressed in black hats and coats, *peyes* whirling wildly.

> *Remember that*
> *in case you make contact*
> *M–I–B*

Jesse spins on his right heel, my dervish, then extends

his arms and struts across the stage, waving his arms and shoulders. Mr. Hollywood himself.

When he's finished, Jesse bends over and, with his right arm across his waist, takes a bow. Then he removes his hat and shades and flashes a smile at me, his mother, a special smile. And there is applause for my son, the kosher ham, who has no stage fright. Jesse has confidence that life is kind, that he will be loved.

"Hey, kid, you got talent," Arnie Keller announces over the microphone. "Know how to get to Carnegie Hall? Take the A train."

My very own grandson, my mother murmurs to herself. When she thought there'd be none. Jesse, named after her baby brother, taken away with her parents, Yom Kippur 1942. *Baruch Hashem.*

My father rushes up to the stage. "Yossileh!" he cries out, then raises Jesse high into the air. The boy flies like an angel. My father toasts their friends of over fifty years. "*L'Chaim!*"